yf

SR

BL

FB

Iq

IH

PH

MAY YOU ENJOY THIS BOOK

DO *NOT* REMOVE THE "DATE DUE" CARD FROM THIS POCKET

Books may be returned to the Main Library, the branches or bookmobiles regardless of where they were checked out. Please return books promptly so that others may enjoy them.

THE PUBLIC LIBRARY
OF DES MOINES, IOWA

D1562653

The Portland Murders

By Charles Larson

THE PORTLAND MURDERS
MUIR'S BLOOD
MATTHEW'S HAND
SOMEONE'S DEATH
THE CHINESE GAME

CHAPTER ONE

The Smell of Fear

I

When Nils-Frederik Blixen reached the studio that Friday morning, the sixteenth of October, he was not only ready for the day's battles, he believed he could win most of them.

The autumn air sparkled. The oatmeal-colored smoke that had suffocated Los Angeles since August had given way to a cornflower-blue sky. There was a sharpness in the wind, something storm-spattered and intoxicating. It had almost rained, the paper reported, last night. The weather bureau had recorded a trace of precipitation at the airport for the first time in eight months. Blixen had sensed it. Toward dawn he had dreamed of piloting a train through a pine forest above a deep green river, and had wakened feeling belligerent, engorged, and twenty years younger. He had cooked himself a breakfast of steak and eggs and been rebuked by the apartment house manager for shouting in the shower.

At the main studio gate a guard in an overcoat and earmuffs stood beside an electric heater and blew into his cupped hands. Blixen tapped him a couple of exuberant honks as he swept by, and then pulled over and backed up when the guard flourished a memo slip, to indicate that he had a message. Blixen lowered his window. "James, my boy," he said.

"Well, you look snarky this morning," the guard said. He was a born Californian, perpetually chilled; he huffed into his hands and banged one foot against the other.

"Come to think of it, I *feel* snarky," Blixen replied. "What does that mean, snarky?"

"You know, loose, like you've put it all together there."

"I never felt snarkier in my life."

"Slip me your secret sometime," said the guard. "Maybe my blood's too thin. I just can't seem to get untracked in weather like this." He broke off when a gust of wind caught the memo in his hand and flipped it up the street. "There, what did I tell you?" he declared. "My fingers are so cold I can't even hold onto nothing." He hurried after the memo, but each time he got within retrieval distance, the wind kicked it farther along, and rather than be made a fool of, he brought his arm around in a gesture of disgust and dismissal and returned to the car. "Hell's bells," he said. "Well, it wasn't important. Bo Derek called to say it's on for tonight if you contact her within the next fifteen minutes. That was her private number. I'm only kidding. It was your secretary. You're to go straight down to Projection Room Six. Oh, and your meeting with Mr. Todd has been canceled, because Mr. Todd wants to see the dailies, too. He'll be there. Also be sure to check into your office before you leave because you forgot to sign the preliminary budget on the next episode and after that some Portland lawyer wants you to give a deposition in a murder case."

"Which I'll attend to as soon as I can shake Bo."

"Suit yourself, but that one's legitimate," said the guard.

Blixen sat back. "Really? What murder case?"

The guard shrugged to indicate that they hadn't confided in him, and then scrutinized Blixen. "Weren't you originally from up that way? Maybe they think you're the infamous Slasher."

"The—?"

"The Slasher, the Slasher. The nut who's been killing all those Portland derelicts. Cuts off their genitals? Leaves the Bible verse and the flowers? Except—wait a minute—I'm wrong—I believe they already arrested somebody for that. Hey, you can breathe easy, Mr. B. You've squeaked through again."

"Close one, wasn't it. . . ." At last Blixen cracked his double-jointed thumbs and slipped the automatic shift into drive. "All right, Jim, thanks," he said.

"I could call your girl and have her follow it up if it bothers you."

"Why should it bother me?"

"I don't know, you look a little flushed."

"That's anticipation. I want to see the dailies. First film on the two-parter."

"Oh, this is the big Hawaiian episode you kept shoving back?"

"Until I could find the right director, yes."

"Who'd you get?"

"Roland Phipps."

"You're putting me on," said the guard. "Phipps? Phipps is dead. Or are we talking about two different Phippses? The Phipps I have in mind is the Academy Award winner."

"So is the Phipps I hired."

"Well, for pity's sake," said the guard. "Huh. How the mighty have fallen." He began to color and fidget and cough. "I don't mean *fallen* exactly. I mean—"

"Right," Blixen said.

"You know how I feel about 'Stagg at Bay,' " said the guard. "This is the best detective series on the air, in my opinion. I'm your biggest fan."

"You just can't understand why a two-time Academy Award-winning director would want to waste time on episodic TV."

"Exactly. No—"

"Let me tell you he was a hard nut to crack. I sat on that man's doorstep for two weeks before he even asked who I was."

The guard motioned a gaggle of dress-extras in long gowns and tiaras through the gate. "So how did you break him down?"

"I promised him certain privileges. Director's cut plus final cut. Complete casting authority. Twenty-eight location days."

"Twenty-eight days! Where's your budget after twenty-eight days?"

"Right down the toilet."

"Then what—"

"We'll make it back on overseas distribution. Release it as a feature. They love Phipps in Europe."

The guard shook his head, and tried to warm his frozen nose between his palms. "I could never produce TV in this town, never," he said. "Not with my spastic colon."

"Oh, you'd get used to it," Blixen said. "In two years' time you'd never know you had a colon."

The phone in the booth rang, and Blixen gunned his motor, and said: "If that's Room Six, tell them I'm on my way."

"Good luck," the guard called, sticking his hands in his armpits and watching the car disappear up the clotted, colorful studio street with a look of the saddest compassion on his face.

II

In Hollywood, fear has a smell as rich and pervasive as meat gone bad. It clings to clothing and hair. It cannot be scrubbed out or washed off. If it were visible it would be mackerel-colored.

Blixen felt it and smelled it and saw it the instant he stepped into Room Six.

There were four men waiting for him in the half dark. His cutter, Jesse Heath, and Jesse's black assistant, Caspar, had positioned themselves on either side of the control panel in the middle of the third row. Arthur Todd, looking every inch the studio head in a blue blazer and white flannel pants, sat on his tailbone in one of the executive armchairs behind them. Down front, Blixen's associate producer, a barrel-chested ex-actor named Barney Lewis, twisted his massive frame to say: "Hey, here's the big chief."

"Gentlemen," Blixen greeted them. "*And* Arthur."

"Get him," said Todd. "He hates me because I'm the dominant male."

Blixen removed his coat and tossed it onto the empty seat next to Todd and sat in the armchair next to that.

"All set? Anyone else coming?"

"Just us masochists," Todd said.

"Arthur," Blixen said, "why don't you give it up, for God's sake? The deed's done. Roland's been hired and he's going to direct a beautiful picture for us."

Todd braced his old knees against the seat in front of him. "Do you know what your major flaw is, Nils?"

"No, Mr. Bones. What's my major flaw?"

"You won't take expert advice. You just go belching along like a tank over a meadow. Guess who called me last night. Your star."

"Which star?"

"Pardner, you've only got one star. I consider the rest of those clods supporting players. I'm talking about your *star*. Stagg. Murphy Smith. Well, the man was virtually in tears. He said that if he'd wanted to be scorned and humiliated, he could have let Jack Warner sign him back in the sixties. He said that not only is Roland Phipps dictatorial, he is also slower than molasses, and furthermore what Phipps knows about film you could put on the head of a pin and have room enough left over for the Lord's Prayer in six languages."

"Isn't that interesting," Blixen mused.

"Oh, don't pretend to be so surprised. I warned you when you started this—"

"I meant," Blixen said, "isn't it interesting that Murphy called you instead of me."

"He can't talk to you."

"Because I won't take expert advice?"

"Because you won't take expert advice."

"Expert advice, Art," Blixen said, "is what a shoe clerk gives Lasorda after the Dodgers lose."

"Except that you're not dealing with shoe clerks now, are you? Murphy Smith is a stage-wise—"

"Murphy Smith," Blixen interrupted, "is a self-destructive, insecure, aging child whose constant nightmare is that some adult will wake up to the fact that he can't act! Of *course* he's afraid of an Academy Award-winning director! And the next time the star calls, would you please refer him to the producer? Now can we get on with this business?"

Todd sighed and rested his chin on his steepled fists and shut his eyes.

"Here we go," Blixen said.

"Uh," said Jesse Heath, "there's just one slight hitch. No sound."

"No? Why not?"

"There's no track. The lab didn't send a track."

In his husky Mississippi voice, Caspar said: "We tryin' to trace it down now, Mr. Blixen."

"Shall we run her anyway?" Jesse asked.

"Please."

Caspar activated the intercom to the projection room and leaned over and whispered into it: "Go, Alex."

Blixen settled deeper into his chilly seat. "How many reels do we have?"

"One reel," Jesse answered.

The lights dimmed.

"Hold it," Blixen murmured.

Caspar leaned over and whispered: "Hold it, Alex." He then sat back and patted the back of his neck dry with his handkerchief.

The lights came up again; the smell of old meat sweetened the air.

"One reel?" Blixen asked.

"This director ain't what you call fast," Caspar said. "Is he?"

Blixen leaned his head against the cracked leather back of his chair and contemplated the leprous ceiling.

Above them the projectionist's amplified voice said: "Men, I'm off at noon. Shall we press on here or what?"

"Press on," said Blixen.

"Press on, Alex," Caspar whispered into his intercom.

Once again the lights dimmed. The leader marks flickered by, and they were looking at a sallow lad in white shorts who picked his nose and whacked the silent jaws of a clapboard shut. Words on the slate read: PROD 3817—DIR. PHIPPS, CAM. FROST. SC 1—TAKE 23.

"Take *what?*" Barney Lewis exclaimed.

"Twenty-three."

"Well—but—!"

"Will everybody be still now," Arthur Todd said, "because I don't want to miss one precious bit of this."

The camera had begun a snail's-paced pan leftward across a rock wall alive with lizards, over the edge of a shattered canyon into a sea of air as clear as a new glass marble. On and on the pan went, past a bird that floated like a thistle on the thermals, beyond range after range of mountaintops flaring against the low sun.

In a querulous voice, Todd said: "Where are we anyhow?"

"Garden Island," replied Barney Lewis. "They've—"

"I mean in the script."

"Oh, this is where the Hawaiian kid apologizes to the gods for killing the guy and Stagg comes up to talk him out of suicide."

"I thought they apologized to the gods at sunrise."

"They do."

"Is *that* sunrise?"

"Isn't it?"

"You know what that is?" Jesse Heath put in. "That's sun*set*."

"It *is* sunset," Todd said. "Why, that rinkidink has been out there all day, burning up film like it was celluloid, and when he does print a take, it's in defiance of all dramatic—"

Blixen put a hand on Todd's arm to quiet him, lost in the trickery of the shot, the brilliance of the conception. The pan had swept over most of Kauai, a full three hundred and fifty-nine degrees, to end on a close-up of the actor who played the Hawaiian kid, to pull focus without the loss of a moment's definition, to take an awed look at two mad eyes in an exhausted face. The haunted young mouth mimed a timeless Polynesian chant.

"Wow," Caspar whispered.

Shaken, Blixen said: "Well, Arthur? What do you think of them apples?"

"What apples? It isn't even original. Mark Rydell did it better in *The Fox*."

"Don't you touch a foot of that sequence, Jesse," Blixen said. "No, sir."

"You're all overreacting, every one of you," Todd muttered. But his heart wasn't in it.

The rest was spinach. Coverage of Stagg clambering up the cliff. The boy threatening to jump and finally the attempted leap, the last-second lunge by the stunt man to grasp the boy's arm and hold on. The two dangling down the cliff face. The laborious haul to safety.

"Flare on the two-shot," Barney Lewis warned.

The signal light on the telephone blinked. Caspar lifted the receiver and said: "Yeah."

"The close-up isn't too shabby, Jess," Blixen said. "Skip the two."

"Well, he's got a funny little move in there, around the rock. It'll jump."

"Let it."

"Mr. Blixen?" Caspar said. "Excuse me? Call for you."

"Who from?"

"Who from, sugar?" Caspar asked into the phone, and then covered the receiver and said: "Long distance. Portland, Oregon. Some lawyer."

"Oh-ho-ho-HO," Arthur Todd grunted. "Here come de judge. You can run, Nils, but you can't hide. Ask Jean Valjean."

"Give it here, Casp," Blixen said. "I know what it's about." He leaned over the seat in front of him and accepted the phone from Caspar and said: "Operator, this is Nils Blixen. Put the Portland party on, will you?"

The reel had ended; the lights rose. "If they switch you to somebody named Javert," Todd said, "hang up." He sank back, laughing and choking.

Blixen massaged the deep horizontal lines in his brow while the seconds ticked past. The long-distance wire was replete with spectral conversations. Little lives leaking out of a twelve-hundred-mile umbilical cord. Blixen had not been home in thirty years. Los Angeles, that smog-encased Unidentified Flying Object, had become his home instead. Abroad, it was Beverly Hills he missed. When he thought of Portland at all, he remembered a sky so low it could be touched, gray rain, silver thaws—

"Hello there!" someone cried faintly. "Nils Blixen?"

"Hello—"

"Am I speaking to Mr. Nils-Frederik Blixen, formerly of Portland, Oregon?"

"You are. Who is this, please?"

"Mr. Blixen, my name is Duffield. I'm an attorney up here? McManus and Duffield?"

"Could you talk a little louder, Mr. Duffield? I can barely hear you."

"How's that?"

"You still sound very muffled."

"I'll shout. Is that better?"

Resigned, Blixen said: "Yes—go ahead."

"I understand you were born and raised in Portland, Mr. Blixen. Is that correct?"

"It is."

"Attended the public schools?"

"Beaumont and Grant, yes."

"Graduated from Grant in nineteen fifty—"

"Yes. Excuse me, what—"

"I believe there was a girl in your class named Karen Chaplin, C-H-A-P-L-I-N. Is that right?"

Low skies, gray rain, silver thaws—and all the long walks home through the yellow autumn afternoons. All the bare-legged girls in their plaid skirts and their sweaters and their books pressed against their breasts. The fresh mystery of them. The piles of wet leaves waiting in the gutters to be burnt. The clatter of the jalopies. The far shouts. The unbearable, ineffable burden of October.

"Hello?" Duffield said.

"Hello."

"Did you hear my—?"

"I'm sorry. Karen Chaplin. Yes, she was in my class." ·

"And when did you last see Miss Chaplin?"

"June, nineteen fifty. I—we attended a graduation party. I left for California the next day."

"Where was this party held, sir?"

"Where was it *held?* Why should you care?"

"Beg pardon?"

Blixen said: "Mr. Duffield—I cling to a number of old-fashioned radical ideas. I believe in the Brotherhood of Man, can you imagine that? I think that minorities have a right to dissent. I applaud the *Miranda* decision. And I really doubt the wisdom of continuing a blind interview like this without having my own lawyer beside me. Now I understand that you wanted me to give a deposition in a murder case—"

The room had grown still. Barney Lewis's eyes were wide as a cat's.

"—and that's fine," Blixen continued, "I'll be happy to depose for you until the cows come home—provided I've been warned, sworn, and advised first. Fair enough?"

"More than fair," Duffield agreed, "except that I'm not asking you to depose to anything. What I was *trying* to do was poke around in your memory without leading you. But if—"

"Memory of what? The graduation party?"

"Of the party, yes."

"Where does this murder come in?"

Abruptly a new voice, a woman's, said: "Very well, that's enough. It isn't working. Let's regroup."

"Did I blow it?" Duffield asked.

Thunderstruck, Blixen shifted the receiver to his other ear. "Who was that! Is there somebody else on this line?"

"Nils?" said the female voice. "Hi. It's Karen."

Once, in his preteens, on a dare, Blixen had walked into a vacant house in the dead of night, and had talked to the ghosts there. When he'd walked out again, his best friend, Clement Gompers, had asked him what the ghosts had said. But he couldn't remember. Well, Clement had persisted, they sure must have scared you, you sure look goofy, what did *you* say? Oh, Blixen replied, we just talked.

"Can you hear me, Nils?"

"I really don't believe this," Blixen said. *"Karen?"*

"Hi."

Jalopies and far shouts and the cramp and cut of cinders through the paper-thin soles of his track shoes. A heatless sun glows over the Grant Bowl. The day is windy; his lungs burn; he is on the third lap of his daily two-mile run, and here she jogs onto the track, headed the wrong way. As they intersect, he tells her so. "Wrong way, dum-dum."

A quarter mile later, they intersect again. "This is the way I prefer," she says, "dum-dum."

Around and around in his mind she trots, plugging on in her billowy shorts, kicking the cinders back at him every quarter mile, the way she prefers.

"—by half," Karen said.

"I'm sorry?"

"I say, this is what comes of trying to be too clever by half."

Duffield said: "It was my fault entirely. Perhaps I can clarify the situation."

"I truly hope so," Blixen said.

"Well, let's have a fling at it," Duffield said. "I was seated here talking to my client, Ms. Chaplin, whom you already know, and who should drop in but a representative of the Portland police, Detective C. R. Flower."

"Power," said a third Portland voice.

"Power," repeated Duffield. "I do apologize. Anyway—"

"Mr. Duffield," Blixen said, and had to clear his throat. "Mr. Duffield?"

"If you're about to object that this is illegal," interrupted Duffield, "it isn't. We're not taping or anything."

"You'd hear a beep if we were taping," Detective Power said. "In fact—"

Sharply Karen said: "Oh, Floyd, stop it! Everybody just shut up for a minute!" Silence descended. "Thank you. Nils, you're angry. You have a right to be. I'm angry, too. I argued and argued against this nonsense. But in Floyd's defense, I assure you he was only trying to help."

"Indeed I was," said Duffield.

Again Blixen had to clear his throat. "Help—who? You?"

"I hope you're ready for this, Nils," Karen said. "I have just been accused of murder."

Power said: "That's simply not accurate, Miss Chaplin."

"Oh, isn't it? Do you deny that you came charging over not ten minutes ago like a Nazi gauleiter—"

"I do deny it. I needed to talk to you. I'd heard you were visiting this office, so I—"

"I suppose I can confer with my own attorney if I choose to?"

"You can. The question is why you choose to today."

"I'll *tell* you why!" Karen said. "Because the Portland police, in their wisdom, have seen fit to prejudice every reporter in town against—"

"Not true. The police—"

Blixen roared "QUIET!" so ringingly that Arthur Todd crushed his newly unwrapped cigar all over his flannel lap.

Again a silence descended.

Refilling his lungs, Blixen said: "Now. First, I want to know who else is on that line. FBI? CIA? Barbara Walters? Who?"

"Nobody else," Karen said.

"Second—both men hang up."

"Well—" Duffield began.

"You hang up, or I hang up," Blixen said. "Your line's overloaded. You sound like the head in Senor Wences's box."

"You heard him, hang up," Karen said.

At last two receivers clicked.

"There we go," Karen said clearly. "Of course the one you ought to be talking to, Nils, is Detective Hitler here—" Her voice diminished as she turned her head, evidently to address Power. "But perhaps Der Führer will allow me to fill in some of the background?"

"It's your quarter," Power said in the distance.

"He says it's my quarter," Karen told Blixen, "so I'll take advantage of that until he slaps the cuffs on me. Now I'm not sure how much of this business the L.A. papers have covered—"

"Don't tell me you're the derelict-murderer—"

"Well, no, actually I haven't been charged with those yet. No, this is the Case of the Butchered Skeleton. Have you read about that?"

"Not a word."

"Do you remember Coco DeForrest's graduation party? We were all going out to the Oaks, but it rained so we stayed at her place instead? Do you remember the mess alongside the house?"

Frowning, Blixen said: "Where they planned to pour the new driveway—"

"They did pour it," Karen said. "The next morning. Unfortunately they poured it over a dead body."

Blixen blinked. "I don't understand—"

"There was a man buried there."

"Under the—?"

"Yes, and I suppose he'd have been there yet if Agnes hadn't decided—"

"Who's Agnes?"

"Coco's mom, Agnes."

"Of course. I'm sorry. Go ahead."

"I was just going to say that Agnes finally decided the house was too big for Coco and her. Gil had died years ago—Gil was Coco's dad—"

"Yes—"

"—so Agnes sold and the new owners dug up part of the driveway to put in a swimming pool and there he was. At least there his bones were—"

Exasperated, Blixen said: "*Whose* bones, Karen? One of the construction—"

"Sophocles Kanaris'."

Inside Blixen, sudden disgust heaves like the scum in a volcano's crater. The taste of vomit rises in his nose; a hot voice hisses Greek imprecations. He is on his belly in the DeForrest rose garden and this yo-yo in the bib overalls is kicking him.

"Did you say something?" Karen asked.

"I—no."

"Sophocles was that foul-mouthed gardener the DeForrests employed. That half-witted degenerate."

"I remember."

"Everybody assumed he'd gone back to Greece. He worked around the DeForrest place on the day of the party and then he just vanished. Apparently some crony of his put in a Missing Persons report, but he never turned up. Anyway, the police lab figured out how old the bones were and how long they'd been in the ground, and then they checked the dental work and it was Sophocles."

"How was he—"

"He'd been stabbed with a butcher knife. The blade was still there, under the ribs."

"God in heaven."

"Well, it puts everybody who was at the party in a kind of an equivocal position, Nils, doesn't it? Me more than the rest of you —but all of us to some extent. I mean, he was horsing around there all day long, and then he was in his grave when the concrete was poured the next morning at eight. We were the last ones to see him alive."

"But the implication's ridiculous! Nobody at that party had any reason to—"

"Ah," Karen interrupted. "Now there the cheese starts to bind. According to Agnes DeForrest, I for one had a pip of a reason."

Suddenly his mind's computer disgorges the scene. He smells sweat and roses. He shouts: "Karen!" Crimson-faced, mad as a wet hen, she is whacking and spitting at the gardener pressing her to the ground. She defends herself strenuously but in utter silence; she is not the swooning kind. It infuriates Blixen, for some reason. After he has galloped to her rescue, and fought for her honor, and been bloodied for it—after Sophocles has scuttled off into the night —Blixen yanks her to her feet and demands to know why she hadn't screamed for help the second Sophocles had attacked her. He cradles the back of her round skull in the palm of his hand, and shouts at her, fiercely protective. But she won't answer him. She knocks his hand aside and marches out of the garden, across the lawn, into the house, dress torn, head erect.

"But maybe you don't recall my little contretemps—"

"I do recall it."

"Well, Agnes DeForrest claims that after Sophocles tried to diddle me, I ran into the kitchen where all the knives were and yelled all kinds of threats and—"

"It doesn't matter *what* you yelled. There's a world of difference between threat and deed. In any case, you didn't even come back out to the garden. You went on home. Didn't you?"

"Yes, I did, but the police theory is that Sophocles was murdered later that night, after the party broke up—after we'd all left, so—"

"But if that's true, wouldn't Mr. and Mrs. DeForrest have heard something?"

"They'd left, too. Apparently there was a terrible scene when Mr. DeForrest came home from work. Coco said the man just went berserk when he saw the mess we'd made. So he checked into a motel, and Agnes took Coco downtown to the Benson. Whereupon I am supposed to have slunk back and done my dark deed unobserved and unmolested."

"Which means that Sophocles must have slunk back, too."

"Yes."

"And how do the police explain that inexplicable move?"

"They don't. They keep asking *me* to explain it. Of course, I've told Detective Hitler here a thousand times that I spent the entire night with you. But he—"

The click and the sudden drain on the line revealed Power's return. "Back again, do you mind?"

"I'll hang up now," Karen said.

Power's voice strengthened. "Well, Mr. Blixen?"

"Well what?" Blixen demanded. "You heard her. We were together."

"From when until when?"

"All night. Until seven or eight in the morning."

"Where?"

"At her home."

"Where were her parents?"

"Out."

Power said: "And you'd be willing to swear to all this in a court of law?"

"Certainly."

"I'll need a signed statement to that effect. Will you come up here or shall I send someone down to you?"

"When would this have to be done? I expected to fly to Honolulu on Monday."

"Where would you stay in Honolulu?"

"Probably at the Kahala."

"I'll have a man at the Kahala Hilton Monday night. How's that?"

"I'll be expecting him."

"Goodbye, Mr. Blixen."

Once more the line faded. "Nils?" Karen's voice grew quieter. "Goodbye. Thank you."

III

Above his head, etched into the low brown projection room ceiling, there was a watermark that resembled Cuba. Someone—Caspar—stood in the projection room door. A horn blatted to command silence on the studio streets and a calico cat bumped and purred against Caspar's ankle. Caspar offered the cat a broken pretzel, which it disdained.

"That it, you guys?" asked Alex's amplified voice.

Blixen nodded. Jesse Heath touched his intercom button and said: "Go, love. Thank you."

"Thank *you*."

Beside Blixen, Todd chuckled and stretched and felt his fly to make sure his zipper was zipped. "My word, radio," he said. "What a joy that was, wasn't it?"

Blixen looked at him.

"Radio," Todd said.

"I heard you."

"Joe Penner," Todd said fondly, "Jack Pearl, well, they were before your time. Fibber McGee and Molly. Remember the closet? Or those phone calls, my word. The phone would ring, and old Molly she'd answer and she'd say, 'Hello? Broke its *back!* Burned? *Forty* of them? Goodbye,' and all this time, Fibber would be sputtering and finally he'd say, '*Who* burned?' and Molly in that casual voice would tell him that old Mrs. Brown was never going to buy any more secondhand books because they went to pieces the minute you opened them, cracked their spines, and she'd tossed the whole lot into the fire." Todd shook his head. "Oh, how I loved those programs."

"Arthur," Blixen said, "would you like to hear what my one-sided telephone conversation was about?"

"If you care to tell me."

"I don't care to tell you."

"Tell me," Todd said.

Blixen sighed and pulled himself to his feet. "Jess," he said, "see if you can run that track down, will you?"

"Yes, sir," Jesse replied.

Blixen clapped Caspar on the back when he passed him in the doorway, and scratched the calico cat's flat forehead, and strolled across the alley and down the studio street.

Todd, woefully out of shape, was panting by the time he caught up. "Where are you headed, Nils?"

"Back to the office."

"I'll come with you."

Several of the companies had broken for lunch. Two World War One doughboys in bloody bandages escorted a number of bald, green Venusian girls toward the commissary. A group of electricians threw frisbees in the forecourt of a sham theater and shouted terrible threats at an interfering dog. The sky had grown lower; by Monday the smog would be killing its quota of weak-lunged pensioners again.

"Nippy," Todd said and shivered. He thrust his hands into his pants pockets. "Going to Honolulu, eh?"

"Going to Honolulu," Blixen said.

"Well, I appreciate that. This is a business like any other business after all. Phipps has cost this studio a fortune. You give him hell." Coins jingled in the old man's pocket. He coughed fiercely, sucked at his teeth.

"Oh, spit it out, Arthur," Blixen said.

"What sort of a police statement are you supposed to make?"

"It's none of your business."

"Is it the studio's business?"

"No."

"Boards of Directors tend to take a different stance on that," Todd said and extended an arm to bar Blixen's way when he put his foot on the first of the Administration Building steps. His eyes bored into the younger man's. "So don't you double-talk me, boy. If you're in trouble, you let me help."

"I'm not in trouble."

"This lawyer just called to chat about the weather?"

The breeze wafted a rich odor from the commissary kitchen. Roast lamb.

"Arthur," Blixen said, "I am not in trouble. A mistake has been made. That's all. Let go of me."

Todd lowered his arm. "Judas Priest," he murmured, "what a fool you are," and turned on his heel and rolled in his sailor's gait up the street toward the parking lot.

CHAPTER TWO

Scene of the Crime

I

Blixen's secretary, Miss Firebush, had opened the cock on the steam radiator to its outermost limit, left a snowstorm of notes among the plastic hippos on his desk, and gone to lunch. The room shimmered. The window frames, painted shut, would not yield to Blixen's banging. He blew on his stung knuckles, and then doffed his coat, loosened his tie, subdued the radiator, and sat wetly in his swivel chair. He scanned the first of his notes and threw the lot into his wastebasket. He signed his preliminary budget. He reformed his disarranged hippos into a Roman phalanx. Heavy-chested, mouths agape, they swaggered across their blotter world.

Blixen rested his head in his hands.

II

Alameda Drive dangles like a necklace along the hilltops in Northeast Portland. On this cool 1950 Friday afternoon, it's still a very desirable area, although cracks are beginning to appear. Pressure has extruded more and more Negro families out of the Albina ghettos, squeezed them up Ainsworth, Killingsworth, up Fremont. It would never have happened in the halcyon days. The 1920s brochures had been unequivocal: people of undesirable colors or kinds prohibited.

Still, blacks are rare on Alameda Ridge, where the DeForrests live. No real estate agent in his right mind would show one through a marketable house. The Chinese Wall has not yet been broached; the streets are as safe as the music.

Listen to the music.

Goodnight, Irene. Third Man Theme. Mule Train. Mona Lisa. The white upper middle-class children sag in each other's arms, inch and shuffle across the polished living room floor. There is punch in a cut-glass bowl on a sideboard, but no one drinks it. Nils-Frederik Blixen has no partner. He is not used to beer and has become quite drunk. He tastes a bit of the punch on the end of an extended little finger. A girl's laughter ripples over the hot room. Coco's laughter. Coco is younger than the rest of them, a very recent seventeen. She presses her belly against her partner, who is one of the MacVicar twins. John? Mickey? Nils can't tell; both boys have open farmer faces, apelike arms, buck teeth. They are from Woodburn. Why Coco enjoys them so, no one can imagine. Opposites must attract. Ever since grammar school, Coco has been called the Duchess. There is something royal about her long legs. Her black eyes, slightly crossed, lend her an innocent air. But she is not innocent. Any usher who has ever worked the balcony in the Hollywood Theater can attest to that. Nils winks at her and she sticks her tongue out at him and jiggles her breasts. Her hair has been cut into the shape of a prize chrysanthemum; black petals curl over her glazed eyes. She is on the very brink of life. High school ended yesterday. Her breasts swing and tremble under her blouse and something swamplike rises in Nils Blixen, grips and scares him. He wants to stride across the floor, throw the MacVicar twin out the picture window, bear Coco to the hardwood, pumping like an air gun, bruise and bloody and terrify her. He is afraid to blink, to breathe; the slightest tremor will cause him to soil himself. He stands stock-still and multiplies figures in his head.

The record ends. The crisis ends as well. Shaken, Blixen leaves the room. Behind him the girl laughs at his back.

In the enormous kitchen, Mrs. DeForrest uses a foot-long butcher knife to slice cooked liver for a young Pomeranian-Spitz named Tiger. Yippy, sharp-toothed beast. Twice he has nipped Nils on the ankle. At night, Nils often dreams of killing him. Mrs. DeForrest manipulates the knife deftly. She has the largest hands Blixen has ever seen. Six feet tall or more, wide-hipped, narrow-chested, she should be repellent, but her blue eyes are so uncertain that Blixen feels sorry for her. He notices now that her powdered *puffy old cheeks are wet. She brushes at the tears and pulls her jaw down in a comic moue. "Onions," she says.*

He says yeah, but he sees no onions. He doesn't want to get involved. He bypasses the slavering dog and clatters down the steps to the cellar landing and out through the screened back door to a broad emerald lawn. Or to what used to be a broad emerald lawn. A broad ravaged lawn now. A number of things have contributed to the disaster. The cracked asphalt driveway that had abutted the house since its construction has been ripped out, and the new concrete one will not be poured until tomorrow, which means that the house is flanked by a sea of mud. Barrow wheels have carved raw gashes through the tough brilliant grass shoots, and backhoes have deposited mountainous boulders on top of Mr. DeForrest's sweet peas. Mr. DeForrest has not yet seen the mess. He will not be happy about it. He will rave in the manner of adults. It crosses Blixen's mind that this may be what Mrs. DeForrest's tears forecast, but he dismisses the notion as farfetched. It is more likely, he decides, that she suffers from female problems.

By now the rain has stopped and the fresh Oregon air soon clears his head. He thinks about college. His parents expect him to attend the university at Eugene in September; he expects to leave home long before then. Leaving home has become an obsession. He longs for freedom. He knows to the penny how much a Greyhound ticket to Los Angeles costs. He has the wherewithal. He could leave tomorrow if he chose.

"Cheer up, old man, it can't be as bad as that," someone says, and he wheels to clutch the forearms of the girl who has crept up on him. Her hair is auburn and unfashionable—straight as a string in this Toni-haunted era. His fingers dig into her flesh, but she shows no sign of panic. Young men have little visible effect on Karen Chaplin. Is it aplomb? Disinterest? For four years she has puzzled the male half of the Class of '50. She neither rebels nor conforms. No one can decide whether she's pretty or plain because for some reason she never decorates herself. Outside of school she prefers sweat shirts and blue jeans. She is a gifted athlete. Girls do not high-jump much in 1950; Karen high-jumps in her backyard.

Clement Gompers, who reads Stekel, believes he has the answer. She is a dike, he insists. But Nils Blixen wonders. He does not really like her; he prefers girls who are unmistakably girls. He is pleased by giggles and nylons and lace, makeup and perfume, girlishness. He is a hunter. He worships prey. Some older woman, he thinks, should teach Karen to bat her eyes, to show her claws, to scamper back and forth like a female baboon in heat, uttering high strange cries.

On the other hand—why do her unbatted eyes disturb him?

He looks down at his fingers on her freckled forearms. He feels drunk again. "You scared me out of a year's growth," he says. "Oh. Am I hurting you?"

Karen shakes her head.

Nevertheless he loosens his grip. It is quite late and the dying June day has given a shadowless pearl-pure tone to the city. He remembers a word from his French class, a favorite of Loti's. The word is "crepuscular." "What a drag these dumb parties are," he says. "We ought to clear out, both of us. We could go to my place. We could fix some food. My folks aren't home."

"What time is it?"

"Almost nine."

"Neither are mine by now," Karen says.

It takes his breath away. She folds her arms across her chest and looks at the long muscle that slopes from his neck to his shoulder. As though he were the prey. He has never been so agitated. He has bragged for years in athletic showers of his prowess. But in fact he is a virgin. He can hear his heart pounding in his voice. "When do you want to leave? Now?"

"Yes."

"I hid some beer in the gazebo. I'll dig it up and meet you out front."

Her eyes are unfathomable. She lifts her hand, traces the fleshy curl at the top of his left ear between her thumb and forefinger. She rests her palm against his cheek. A fingertip lies as lightly as a breath in the ear's cavity. She drops the hand and is gone.

The ear play has fixed him like a spaniel pointed at a duck. He sees Clement Gompers drift out of the garage at the end of the driveway, but he cannot seem to untrack himself. Clement slops through the mud to his side.

"Hey, Nils?" Clement says.

Clement is built like a guinea pig who has somehow learned to stand on its hind legs. Clement has doubled his neck size through a weird combination of barbell exercises and overeating. He is both puffy and strong. He anchors the football line at center. He is loyal, dull-witted, dewlapped. He is a secret smoker. His breath reeks in Blixen's nostrils. He has been sneaking a cigarette in the garage.

"Buzz off, animal," Blixen says.

"Huh?" Clement says. "Okay, neat-o." He squints around the backyard. "I'm supposed to take Lucille Epps home. Have you seen her?"

"No, buzz off."

"How about Sophocles?"

Blixen is a sometime customer of Sophocles, who has sold pornography to generations of Alameda males. Clement is an avid one.

"Will you buzz off?"

"Hey, Lucille?" Clement calls, and tracks an ocean of mud onto the cellar landing and up the steps that lead to Mrs. DeForrest's immaculate kitchen.

"Crepuscular" is no longer the apposite word; night has fallen. A plane snores toward the ten-year-old airport along the Columbia. Blixen's paralysis has left him, although his extremities continue to tingle.

The rose garden is located on the far southwestern corner of the DeForrest property. It is a pretty, odoriferous place. A gazebo has been erected in the center of it so that the DeForrests may enjoy the scent and the view on summer evenings. Blixen starts up the gravel path to the gazebo, but stumbles against something and stops to check it out.

He has struck a knee in a wrinkled stocking. He bends a rosebush aside. Lucille Epps blinks miserably back at him. She is round-faced and short-legged. She has been sick. She is pale and ashamed.

"Well, you're a pretty sight," Blixen says. "Are you dying?"

"Oh, I hope so," groans Lucille. "Why did God create beer?"

Blixen thinks it's funny. "Gompers is looking for you. He claims you're his date."

"He does? He is? Is he?" The notion seems to energize her. She gathers together whatever forces she has left; she glares at the

*ground between her hands like a weight lifter psyching himself up,
and surges to her hands and knees.*

*Blixen is repelled by the whole process. He feels that women
should make every attempt to be attractive (he means young
women) and if they cannot or will not, then they should at least
have the grace to remain hidden. Beside him, Lucille huffs and
quivers. She cannot gain any leverage. Blixen would like to help,
but she is not his responsibility.*

"I'll go find Gompers," he says.

"No!"

Her vehemence startles him.

*She shoots him a savage glance. "Do you think I want him to
see me like this?"*

*She clambers somehow to her feet. She gulps air, motions him
aside, brushes at her skirt, and cants off up the path.*

"I'll take a nap, I'll be fine," she assures the night.

*Hands on his hips, Blixen scowls after her. Gratitude at being
born male dizzies him.*

*It is pitch-dark now. He has to make his way to the gazebo
behind an outstretched arm, and even so he is stung by thorns. He
trips on the gazebo step, falls flat. Absurd. He'll never recover the
beer at this rate. He pats the post beside him, locates the light button. He presses it and is bathed in fairy colors, golds and soft reds
and blues from wrinkled Japanese lanterns. The beer is stuffed
into the cracks of a leather sofa; he finds his treasure, and is trying
to pry the cap off one of the bottles when the lanterns are extinguished.*

Someone sniggers.

*It unmans him. Shock spits across the backs of his knees, up his
spine. He is a true-crime addict. On the muggy morning of August
4, 1892, Lizzie Borden had stood at the top of the stairway in her
father's home, watched the Irish maid open the door to old An-
drew, and had chuckled like that. Behind her lay the slaughtered
body of her stepmother. Ahead lay parricide. Nils Blixen has
heard Lizzie's lazy laugh in more than one nightmare. The sound
is low and feminine; the laughter castrates; the knife kills. It is interesting that he thinks "knife," rather than "axe." He thinks of a
bright butcher knife slicing liver for a yippy dog.*

The words take a paragraph to tell but the horror is much

swifter, as brief as the flight of an arc across a spark plug. Within seconds he is himself again. The chuckler, he realizes, is not Mrs. DeForrest but Coco.

The girl is outlined in the gazebo entryway. She murmurs something that he can't quite catch, and then adds: "Oh, who cares?" and swims toward him. Light from some puzzling source on this stygian night glitters in her eyes. "What's that, beer? Just what I need. Daddy's on his way home. He's also on the warpath."

Her words are slurred, and Blixen perceives that she is drunker than he. It frets him. It excites him.

"Mummie's terror-stricken," Coco adds. "She wants to clutch me to her bosom and flee across the ice. But I vetoed that." Her arms lift. "Dance." It's an unaggressive order. She doesn't leap at him. She waits, passive.

He has forgotten Karen. He takes what is at hand. He closes himself against Coco like a lion descending on an antelope. His hands squeeze her buttocks.

Only then do the sounds from the garden intrude. If lust has narrowed his vision, anxiety has pricked up his ears. Someone is panting out there. Blows thud. He inclines his head sharply. There are no words, but the panting is feminine, furious. He smells sweat and roses. He shouts: "Karen!" and storms battleward. Karen whacks at the gardener atop her in utter silence. Blixen is both noisier and more accurate. He hauls at the slick, grimy, gardener-jaw. The man rolls aside, scrambles to his feet. Froth from his wheezing mouth sprays Blixen's face. The fist he aims at Blixen's head strikes the breast-bone instead. Coco has either swooned in the gazebo, or, wisely, is faking it. A shoe stabs into Blixen's kidney, thorns rake his face. He presumes he is due to die here. Strange Samarra. But by the time he extricates himself from the rosebush, Sophocles already is scuttling away. Blixen forgoes pursuit and instead yanks Karen to her feet. "Why didn't you scream!" he shouts, and cradles the back of her round skull in his numb palm, protective, proprietary, raving . . .

III

"Oh, dear, you're *in!*"

Miss Firebush uttered a wild whoop and splayed her hand over her reddening chest. She had sped halfway across his office before braking. She often used his private washroom at noon. It was an unspoken perk. "I should have buzzed. I never dreamed. How awful. Well." She changed direction and churned back toward the doorway.

"Muriel," Blixen said.

"Yes, sir." Pivoting, she delved into her gray hair for a pencil, then blinked at her empty free hand. "I don't have my book."

"You won't need your book," Blixen said. "I was simply going to say that if you'd like to use my toilet—"

He had chosen the wrong word. It transfixed her like a misthrown javelin. "Your? Why, no. Why, I've never. I'll get my book."

"You get your book," Blixen agreed wearily.

To his surprise, she was back at once. She bustled over to the sofa, sat down, crossed her knees. Her calf muscles contracted each time she reprimanded her wayward bladder. Dismissal was useless; she would not be satisfied until he had dictated something.

Blixen said: "All right, I want to go to Honolulu on Monday—"

"Monday," muttered Miss Firebush. "Economy?"

"First class."

"The studio has a rule—"

"First class."

"First class," muttered Miss Firebush, and drew nervous faces in her margins while Blixen rotated in his swivel chair to gaze out the fogged windows. Miss Firebush stood it as long as she was able, and then cleared her throat.

Blixen swung back. "Cancel that." He nudged the leading bull hippo broadside. The hippo fell onto its back, lay foolishly in the path of the onrushing phalanx. "I want a seat on the next flight to Portland instead."

Miss Firebush raised her eyebrows.

"Round trip," Blixen continued. "Leave the return date open."

"You're dubbing this afternoon," Miss Firebush warned.

"Barney can handle it. Thank you, Muriel."

Miss Firebush nodded, closed her book, left the room graciously, and ran like the wind for the ladies'.

CHAPTER THREE

I Swear I Don't Know What's
Happening to This City

I

From the air, at least, Blixen thought, the city looked the same.

Leaning against his seat belt, he watched the dark earth bloat and twist below him. Above the cloud cover, the afternoon had been mint-bright. Here they descended through sheets of rain into a world as gray as Lapland. On the Columbia, toy-sized motorboats chugged back and forth; cars slipped along glistening streets.

A road flickered past. They were over a runway; wheels struck, bounced, squealed. While the plane lumbered toward the terminal, Blixen gazed at the hoarse air duct over his head and wondered how the dubbing had gone and considered the slender line between impulse and responsibility. What on earth had prodded him into this unplanned operation? Surely not the Proustian echo alone of a clear, young voice, the smell of October smoke, the cut of cinders? He was a realist. The snows of yesteryear always melted, and he knew that. But here he was.

His decision had left Todd stupefied.

The moment that Blixen's intention had been announced, Todd had stomped downstairs to demand an explanation. His wattles never had shaken so fiercely, his face never had been redder. Blixen's obligations, he proclaimed, lay in Hawaii, not Portland. Blixen said he agreed. Then why wasn't he *going* to Hawaii? Blixen replied that he had a statement to make and a friend to reassure and that he would tend to the store in time. First things first, was the way he put it. Well, Todd swore, *somebody* was going to Hawaii, whereupon Blixen had contacted Barney Lewis

in the dubbing room, and ordered him to drop everything and rush to the Islands. Barney Lewis had said he was Blixen's to command, but that he wasn't about to fly steerage, so Todd had been forced to authorize *two* first-class chits. In the end, Todd had confessed himself beaten. He had put his head in his hands and told Blixen that he was too old for this rotten business, that here the studio was crumbling about his ears and no one cared, and in addition to everything else he believed he was getting prostate trouble.

"Sir?"

Blixen jumped. A natty young flight attendant, rebuttoned into her tailored jacket, loomed above him. A yellow slicker dangled over her arm. "Is this yours?"

He had had one once, very like it, when he was ten. It was a sou'wester, but he always had thought of it as a fireman's coat, principally because it had come accompanied by what to him was a long-tailed fireman's hat. Hundreds of Portland kids had dawdled to school in similar costumes, chilled and redolent, splashing through every gutter along the way. Funny pictures and slogans had been printed on the oilskins. One in particular had amused him. HEAVY DATE, it had said, under a cartoon of a fat girl on a scale. A balloon above the fat girl's head had said: "Eek!"

Blixen touched the cool, sticky sleeve. "I don't think it would fit me now."

"This? It wouldn't?"

"I mean the one I—" Blixen stopped. "No, it isn't mine." He showed her his Burberry. "I have mine. Thank you."

He eased past her into the crowded aisle where he and his fellows hobbled in silence toward the front exit, subdued as convicts.

II

If the city had appeared the same from the air as Blixen had remembered it, it looked, from the terminal, as dissimilar as a five-thirty freeway from Sunday afternoon in a hammock.

At the mouth of the unloading ramp, waiting women shrieked incessantly and men battered each other on the biceps and a child threw up on the garish carpet. Any number of persons named

Wjtyusiolpew were advised to contact United Airlines on a white courtesy phone. In 1938, when Blixen had last gazed upon a Portland airport, it had been on Swan Island in the Willamette River and it had had the spurious air of a Howard Hawks movie set. One had drunk soda pop at a wooden counter and listened to the old-timers remember the day in 1927 when Lucky Lindy had circled the city while Mayor George Baker had waved his hat and wept tears of pride on the tarmac below.

Bemused, Blixen allowed the current to eddy him on down a satellite corridor into an agitated pool of shops and services. Buy Oregon. Magazines. Cocktails. Under an arrow pointing to BAG-GAGE and TAXIS, he spied an unoccupied public telephone cubicle, and gained it for himself in a race against an out-of-shape cow-hand. The cowhand flicked him a grin and a finger, and Blixen returned the grin.

PORTLAND, CITY OF.
Police Bureau.
Detective Division.
Homicide.
555 5756.

The bell had rung twice before he pressed his thumb against the cut-off bar. His quarter cannonaded into the return-coin slot. He brooded over the thumb for a second, and then he replaced the phone and opened the Directory to page 128, CENTRAL C-CHALENOR. But the next unmutilated page was 131, CHARLSON S-CHENEY; no Chaplin. He retrieved his quarter, and opted at last for Gompers Clement over Directory Assistance.

The voice that answered the Gompers number was tantalizingly familiar. "Hello."

"Is this Mrs. Gompers?"

"Yes, it is."

"I'm sorry to disturb you, Mrs. Gompers. I was trying to locate your husband—"

"He's not here. Who's this?"

"I'm afraid my name wouldn't mean anything to you. Clement and I used to go to school together years ago, and I've—"

"I'll be darned!" Mrs. Gompers cried. "Nils!"

Blixen stared blankly.

"Aren't you Nils Blixen?"

"Oh," Blixen said, "well, yes. But—"

"Sure! I'd know that voice anywhere! Where *are* you?"

"I'm at Portland International—"

"You don't remember me, do you?"

"I do and I don't," Blixen said. "There's—"

Laughing, Mrs. Gompers said: "It's Lucille."

And now at last the half-forgotten girlish word rhythms fell into place, the chesty tones, the almost nonexistent western *u, shrr* for *sure.* "Lucille!" he said. "Well, how in the world have you been!"

"Oh, just fine, Nils! How have you been?"

"Fine!"

"We see your name on TV."

"Do you?"

"Oh, all the time! How long will you be in town?"

"A few days. I had a call from the Portland police—"

"Really? You, too? Well, I guess you would. We all have. You mean because of the skeleton under Coco's driveway. Did they tell you who it was? It was that vile beastly old poop, what's-his-name—"

"Sophocles."

"Oh, how I detested that man! Clemmie doted on him, can you imagine? I used to say, bud, you'd whistle a different tune if you were a girl, but Clemmie said I was prejudiced. I said, you bet I'm prejudiced, I'm prejudiced against those horny old hands all over me like a coat of paint every time I turn around. And it wasn't just me, either. The man was absolutely insoluble. What do I mean?"

"Insatiable."

"Yes, insatiable. You ask any of the girls. You ask Karen Chaplin. I don't know whether you remember it or not, but Karen got the full treatment that night. Mr. Wonderful caught her in Coco's rose garden, and really, you know—"

"I talked to Karen," Blixen said.

"Oh, you did? When, today? Was she in jail?"

"She was in her lawyer's office."

"See, they want to arrest her because she threatened to kill the old goat, but they're afraid to," Lucille said. "Those Keystone Kops, they take one look at a pile of bones thirty years old and right away they're all Nero Wolfes. Clemmie says there isn't a one of 'em who knows his own ear from a hole in the ground. Karen wouldn't hurt a fly. Anyway, if you ask me, I don't think it was even Sophocles in that grave."

"They should be able to tell by the teeth," Blixen said.

"Oh, *teeth!*" Lucille snorted. "How's Heitkemper going to remember what a certain tooth looked like after thirty years?"

"Who's Heitkemper?"

"Heitkemper?" Lucille said. "*Heit*kemper. You went to Dr. Heitkemper. We all went to him. He filled one of my teeth this morning. He was Sophocles' dentist."

"Is he still *alive?*"

"Well," Lucille said, "he's older than the Peruvian Andes, but, yeah, he's still alive. Sort of. He's still got that same office over on Forty-first. He works for the police all the time. But if that makes him an authority, I'm Annette Funicello. I mean, he's an old dear, Nils, and I love him, but the Michelangelo of the drill he is not. Why couldn't they be an old Indian's teeth out of some burial ground?"

"Because there weren't any old Indian burial grounds on Alameda Ridge."

"All right, why couldn't they be Gilbert DeForrest's teeth? Sophocles wasn't the only man in the world to disappear that night. Gilbert DeForrest disappeared. Him and his temper and his phobias."

"I'm not sure I follow you—"

"Don't you remember how mad Mr. DeForrest was at the party? Yelling and slamming around?"

"Vaguely."

"All right, Coco told me he'd been due to fly east on business that next morning, but he got into this grisly fight with Agnes— that's his wife—"

"Yes."

"So out he storms, goes to a motel or something, and flies east the next day. Maybe. Nobody saw him off. Maybe he never left. He certainly never came back that *I* heard of. You know what we all figured, of course."

"What?"

"Well, that he'd dumped Agnes. I mean, they fought all the

time, they were Catholics, couldn't get a divorce, so what's left? If you're a man, you start a whole new life, and *voilà*."

"Maybe that's what happened."

"And maybe not. Why couldn't that have been him under the driveway?"

"Wrong teeth."

"Oh, you and your teeth."

"Lucille," Blixen said thoughtfully, "how much of that night do you still remember?"

"The night of the party? Not much. Except the beer. I still can't look a glass of beer in the face. Clemmie was just appalled. He found me in the rose garden—"

"That was me," Blixen said.

"What was you?"

"*I* found you in the rose garden. Under a bush. I offered to send Clement out, but you wouldn't let me. You said—"

"Wait, I know, I know! I took a nap. Didn't I?"

"I have no idea."

"Well, I must have, because I was in that big bed of Mrs. DeForrest's when Clemmie woke me up and took me to the Hamburger Hut for a sandwich. And who should be there but Sophocles. Well, first crack off the bat, the old fool slipped me a pinch that turned my bottom blue for a week. I told Clemmie to hit him, but he said it was a compliment and to just shut up, so I did."

"And about what time was this?"

"Oh, this was pretty late. When did the Hut close in those days? Midnight?"

"So Sophocles was still alive at midnight. . . ."

"Sure. He left just after you showed up."

"Me?"

"Wasn't that you?" Lucille asked. "Somebody came in—one of the gang—I thought it was—oh! No, you know who came in, Mickey MacVicar! Poor baby—"

Blixen's brain reeled. "Why poor?"

"Mick's dead."

"Oh, I'm sorry—"

"Yes, Mick was killed in Korea. Missing in action. Well, for heaven's sake, there's a *third* body that just vanished! Anyway, he

was alive then, of course, and he wandered in and said something
to Sophocles and out they both went."

"And that was the last you saw of Sophocles?"

"Yes, because I'd started to feel better with a little food inside
me, and I wanted to do something, so me and Clemmie and another kid drove down to Seaside! Can you imagine? Daddy threatened to disown me, but he never did."

"Mick didn't go? To Seaside?"

"No, no, Mick just took off Friday night and joined the Army. I
never was close to Mick. I never did see Mick again. John called
us when he got the news. About the death. Terrible. It nearly an-
nihilated John. It certainly gave him religion. He quotes Scripture
until you could scream. You remember how close those two always were. John hasn't been the same man since."

"I suppose John went back to Woodburn—"

"No, as a matter of fact, John took up medicine. He's a psychiatrist. He lives in Portland Heights. Twenty-four twenty-three
Broadway Drive. He'd love to talk to you. Call him."

"I'll check you all out before I leave. . . . Let's see, you and
Clement are on Southeast Twentieth. . . . How about Coco?"

"Coco and her mom have a house on Brazee. She's in the book.
But, wait a minute, why don't we all get together here tomorrow
night! Don't you want to see Karen again?"

"Yes."

"Six-thirty, seven o'clock? I'll invite John, too. Oh, isn't this exciting? We'll have a reunion. We can sit around and shoot little
glances at each other like they did in the B movies, and maybe
Charlie Chan will rush in with Number One son, and point a
finger and say 'you commit murder!' Gosh, I wish Clemmie'd been
here! He'll just be sick he missed you, Nils. Can he call you when
he gets in? If it's not too late?"

"By all means. I'll be at the Hilton."

"I'll tell him. . . . You take care now—"

"You, too, Lucille."

Behind Blixen, the cowhand continued to shuffle and pick his
nose and beam. Blixen pressed the transmitter bar down, pon-
dered the notes he had made, and then again looked up the number for Directory Assistance.

Over Blixen's shoulder, the cowhand said: "Sweetheart, I absolutely got to use that phone. Now do you wanna give way there, or should I come in and swarm all over you?"

"You come in and swarm all over me," Blixen said. He contacted a pleasant male operator and obtained Karen's number and tried it, but hung up after six rings. He rose and bowed the cowhand toward the cubicle. "All yours," he said.

"I'm flat," said the cowhand. "Have you got a quarter?"

"Yes," Blixen said, and walked off and left the other with his finger up his nose.

III

Downstairs, the luggage from United 317 had been unloaded onto an endless band that snaked in and out of the baggage area. Already most of the suitcases had been picked over and retrieved; Blixen's one disreputable grip bounced toward him as diffidently as an unwanted dog; he gathered it in, surrendered its check stub to a black clerk at the exit gate, and followed the arrows to a taxi stand outside. He climbed into the back of the first cab in line, and then sat glowering at the cracked leather on the top of the driver's seat for so long that the driver switched around to face him. "Ah—yes," Blixen said. "Let's do it this way. I want to end up at the Hilton, but we may have a stop or two first. Take Sandy and turn on Fremont."

"You got it," said the driver and activated his meter.

They sped through the encroaching night up a road lined with billboards and cultivated fields. It was all familiar, and it was all different. In Blixen's scabby-kneed youth, 82nd Avenue had been the end of the world. Beyond 82nd had lain only dragons. Now, homes stretched east endlessly into the dusk. Westward, though, Fremont had not changed very much. Except to become narrower, shabbier. By the time they had reached 57th, a faint headache had begun to dance behind Blixen's eyes. He ignored it. He wiped the steam from the side window and saw the passing walls of the Rose City cemetery. His mother and father were buried there. His stillborn older brother lay nearby under a flat stone that bore a single date. BABY BLIXEN, APRIL 9, 1931. As a child, Blixen had haunted the spot, awed by the incomprehensibility of deathday and birthday being the same. In fantasy, he had fashioned an entire life for that small unknown brotherly ghost. Its name was Erik. Its athletic prowess was legend. It was kind, intelligent, strong, protective. It loved him.

48th. 44th. His old lunchroom, the O-So-Good, had metamorphosed into something called Hamburger Patti's. At 41st, they stopped for a light. Across the way, a gracious two-storied brick building loomed against the sky. A school. Beaumont. Blixen leaned forward. "Excuse me—do you have the time?"

"Ten past five."

"Turn right here."

They crawled through the beaded rain down 41st. At the corner, a light shone in a second-story suite over a dry goods store. "Stop."

He got out slowly. Above an entryway between the dry goods store and a shoe-repair shop, a metal sign creaked in the wind. D. HEITKEMPER, D.D.S.—SECOND FLOOR.

This way, Blixen thought, to Brigadoon.

IV

Nothing had altered in thirty years. Not the lightless climb. Not the throaty bump of interior plumbing. Especially not the terrifying smell of anesthetics and fear, tooth powder, cleanliness, crushed silver, drilled enamel.

An overhead bell pinged when he opened the waiting room door and clunked as he closed it. In the room beyond, a burly old man in Levi's and a plaid woolen shirt closed a checkbook and hitched around.

It was Heitkemper, though it was Heitkemper seen at the small end of the telescope, not older so much as reduced. He had always been old. He had taught at the School of Dentistry in Eugene in 1929. He had opened his practice in these two rooms in '32. He had been thirty-two then; he was eighty-one now. "Who's that? What have you got, a toothache?" he asked.

"Hello, Dr. Heitkemper," Blixen said.

The old man stuck a pair of glasses on his nose and hooked his arm over the back of his chair. "Am I supposed to recognize you?"

"Nils Blixen," Blixen said.

"Uh-huh," said Heitkemper, and then: "Well, Jesus Christ!" He shoved the chair back and strode into the waiting room. "Yes, sir, it is! How's that gum trouble?"

"You cured it thirty years ago," Blixen said.

"Let's see."

Blixen opened his mouth.

"Uh-huh," Heitkemper said. "Close."

Blixen closed.

"Well, sit down!" Heitkemper said. "Somebody told me you left Portland."

"I did."

"Where'd you go?"

"Southern California. Hollywood."

"Yeah?" Grinning, Heitkemper poked him toward the tufted couch. "Go on, sit down, sit down, sit down! By God. Hollywood, huh?"

"Doctor, I don't want to take you away from your work—"

"What work? I was paying some bills. Let 'em wait." He plopped down beside Blixen, whapped him on the knee. "I like it when you young squirts come back to see me! I appreciate that." The shrewd old eyes bored into Blixen's. "Even when I'm an afterthought."

"Who said you were an—"

"I'll bet I know why you're in Portland," Heitkemper said.

"Why?"

"Either you read about the skeleton under the driveway or Power called you."

"Spang in the gold. Power called me. Well, an attorney named Duffield called, but I talked to Power, too."

"Hell of a scandal. That's Karen Chaplin's lawyer, Duffield."

"Right."

"Terrible teeth," Heitkemper said, "but he knows his business. Well, he better, for his client's sake. Karen's in trouble. Duffield tell you that?"

Blixen said: "It's serious, then."

"It's critical. I got a pipeline into police headquarters. Power has made his mind up. He means to nail that girl if he dies trying."

Quietly, Blixen said: "Nail her based on what evidence?"

"Motive. Opportunity."

"He can forget opportunity. I've already told him Karen and I were together that night. She couldn't have killed anybody."

"Uh-huh."

"What's that mean?"

"Means uh-huh," Heitkemper said. "Quit working so hard. I'm on your side. If I was the D.A., I wouldn't touch this case. No jury's about to decide for sure what happened thirty years ago."

"But Power can't see that?"

"Power," Heitkemper said and blew his breath out. "Power's got a bee in his bonnet."

"He's also got an alibi staring him in the face. Don't alibis cut any ice with this man?"

"Not much," said Heitkemper. "You want a drink? Little scotch?"

"No, I want to talk about alibis," Blixen said.

Heitkemper sighed. "All right. You be Power. I'm you. I come along and I say, 'Look, this Karen kid's as innocent as a newborn lamb and I can prove it because she and I spent the whole night in question fooling around. Of course it was thirty years ago, and parts of it are too vague to remember now, and I guess she *could* have slipped out while I slept but she wouldn't do that because she's such a sweet chick. And sure I loved her, but that don't make me prejudiced, does it? Corroborating witnesses? Are you nuts? Who asks guests over when you're fooling around?'" Heitkemper wiped his mouth and gazed at Blixen over his cupped hand. "There's my alibi," he said. "How much ice would it cut with *you?* Sure you won't have a snort?"

"No, but you go ahead."

"I believe I will," Heitkemper said, and got up and lumbered into the back office. Liquor gurgled into a glass. "Ah," Heitkemper said, and returned to stand in the doorway, glass in hand.

Jingling his change, Blixen rose, paced to the window, back to the bookcase. "All right," he said. "There are parts I don't remember. The alibi's weak. But so is Power's case."

"That's what I keep telling him."

"Then why—"

"How many cops," Heitkemper interrupted, "have you known well in your lifetime?"

"Well? None."

"They're a funny breed," Heitkemper said. "Especially detectives. They'll all tell you that criminology's a science, but not one in a hundred of 'em *thinks* like a scientist. You know what a good cop depends on most? Intuition. Clues don't solve cases, hunches do. Plus a kind of a mule-stubbornness. Now you take Conrad Power. They saddled two big cases on Connie, and there ain't a single clue worth a fly's toot in either one of 'em. He's supposed to find a killer who stabbed a Greek gardener to death for some unknown reason thirty years ago *and* a nut who goes around chopping up senile old derelicts for no reason at all—"

"I thought the police caught the derelict killer."

"According to Power they did. Some young barber named Flinders. But Flinders's girl friend gave him an alibi and the D.A. wouldn't bring charges." Heitkemper aimed his glass at Blixen. "But here's my point. Connie didn't drop *his* charges. He *knows* Flinders sliced up those derelicts, and he'll keep after him come hell or high water or you name it." Shrugging, Heitkemper finished his drink. "Unfortunately, he feels the same way about Karen Chaplin."

"Then he's a fool."

"No, he's not a fool. He's smart and he's patient. He's like a pit bull with the best dentition you ever laid your eyes on. And the only thing that's gonna unlock those jaws is absolute, irrefutable proof that somebody else stabbed Sophocles Kanaris."

Back at the window, Blixen gazed across Forty-first toward the rain-washed brick school, and tried to pick out landmarks. It seemed to him that the music room had been on this side of the building, on the ground floor, under a pocked, padded ceiling that was supposed to be soundproof—where cracked records had been played and carols sung and where he'd heard his first operatic aria and had become a slave of Lily Pons forever. "Who else hated Sophocles?" he asked.

"Who didn't? Well, hated, maybe that's too strong a word. But he was a bad man. He was a bigot, he was a deadbeat—"

"Did he ever try to stiff you?"

"Tried and succeeded," Heitkemper said. "I cleaned his filthy teeth three times for him and he never paid me a dime for any of it."

Musingly Blixen said: "Doctor—"

"Dwayne."

"Dwayne," Blixen said, "how sure are you that the jaw in that grave belonged to Sophocles Kanaris?"

"One hundred percent," Heitkemper replied. "Why?"

"How is a dental identification arrived at? I mean, does somebody bring you a skull or—"

"Oh," Heitkemper said. "No, it's more a confirming than an identification. It's like fingerprints. You can't make a blind identification from one or two prints, no matter how often it's done on TV. Give the FBI nine or ten prints and they'll check 'em against their records, but even then it's tough. What you need is a name, a guess, somebody who *might* have left the prints. Then you compare. Same thing in dentistry. First somebody says, 'This here *could* have been Yorick, let's find out.' So they locate Yorick's dentist and ask him to measure the jaw against Yorick's X rays and records, and then either confirm or deny."

"Who guessed the skeleton in this case might be Sophocles Kanaris?"

"Conrad Power."

"And Power then contacted you?"

"Nope," Heitkemper said, "first a technician from the state police lab down at Second and Pine dropped in and showed me some photographs and asked me if I recognized the work. I said I sure did. So I got out Sophocles' X rays and later on we both looked at the jaw itself and that was that."

Blixen jammed his fists into his back pockets and stared out at the rain.

"Good try, though," Heitkemper said.

Blixen said: "I wasn't trying anything."

"Sure you were," said Heitkemper. "You want to believe that Power hocussed me somehow, substituted Sophocles' skull for the one in the grave, which would let Karen off the hook and which is not only ridiculous but leaves you higher and drier than ever. I mean, where would Power find Sophocles' skull if not in the grave?"

"Good question," Blixen said.

"Who do *you* think was buried under that driveway?"

"Sophocles Kanaris."

"Well, welcome back from Cloud Nine."

V

"Where to now?" asked the cab driver. "Hilton?"

Slamming his door, Blixen said: "Not yet. Turn around and go back down Forty-first to Klickitat. Then right to Thirty-ninth."

The long dark blocks were somnolent. TV sets bloomed in the corners of lighted living rooms. There would be the aggressive smell of fish frying in half these kitchens on this Friday night. Salmon, more than likely. There would be mashed potatoes and green beans. Lemon meringue pie.

40th.

39th.

"Stop."

Someone was practicing piano scales in the second house from the corner, Blixen's old home. Outside, a potbellied man in a gray raincoat smoked a cigarette while a cocker spaniel squatted under a white birch tree.

"What are you after, some address?" the driver asked.

"Nineteen fifty," Blixen said.

"Oh, you're way off," said the driver. "This here's thirty-three hundred. Nineteen fifty'd be down the hill. I think I know where that is."

"Nobody knows where that is," Blixen said. His eyes stung; he sat back. "Turn left."

"We can't go through here," said the driver. "See the detour sign? I'll have to take Thirty-third. They found a skeleton on Alameda. They blocked off the whole area."

"Turn left anyway."

"Oh, how the money rolls in," said the driver and wrenched his wheel to the left and squeezed between the detour sawhorse and the curb.

They passed Karen's house, still as rakish as her weird parents. Once the Chaplins had painted their front door red. The neighborhood had decided it was another slap in the face, some crazy bohemian yawp. Chaplin was a veterinarian who brewed beer in his basement and served on the school board and believed in One World. His wife, a Ph.D. from Vassar, worked right alongside him, curing cats and winding snakes around her arms. During the war Halloweens, Chaplin took to wearing a Dracula costume and lying in a simple pine box at the side of the driveway with the head of a lighted flashlight in his mouth to make his cheeks bloody. When the trick-or-treaters passed him he would lift himself, groan, and spread his black cape. Blixen's father referred to him as that damned showboat. Blixen himself would plan for eleven months to lead some newcomer down that wondrous driveway. The MacVicar brothers, fresh from Woodburn, had screamed like—

No.

Blixen frowned at the rain-spattered window.

No, the MacVicars had not even moved to Portland until—when? 1949? Long after trick-or-treat days. Yet he remembered a MacVicar shriek on that driveway—

"There, see for yourself," said the driver.

The memory was at the very edge of his mind, no farther from fruition than Adam's finger was from God's on the Sistine ceiling. Himself running. MacVicar shrieking.

"Hey, friend?" said the driver. "Friend? Friend?"

Blixen glanced up.

The driver hung over the back of the front seat. "I don't want no heart attacks in here—"

"I'm not having a heart attack. Why did you stop?"

"We can't get through. I told you."

They had halted at the intersection of 38th and Alameda, where a police barrier stretched from curb to curb. Beyond the barrier, spotlights illuminated the right side of the former DeForrest house. A tent had been erected over the driveway. Lights flickered behind the canvas walls.

Blixen studied the scene. "When was this skeleton found?"

"What's today, Friday? It must have been last Wednesday. He was kilt thirty years ago. They dumped him in a trench and the next day they built this concrete drive over him. They never would have found him if the present owners hadn't of wanted a swimming pool. They dug up the drive and there he was. I swear I don't know what's happening to this city. This town used to be a real nice place to bring up your children in. Since Vietnam, since *Korea,* it's wall-to-wall violence. Skeletons, slashers. Did you hear about our Slasher?"

"Yes."

"Terrible. Here's this flake running around carving up old men. They thought they caught him two, three weeks ago, but he had an alibi and they had to let him go. What a world. You want to head on to the hotel now or what?"

After a moment Blixen said: "Let's head on to the hotel."

The driver flung an arm over the seat, backed into a driveway. "Alibis," he said, "who believes alibis? I mean, your average alibi today isn't worth the paper it's printed on. Why, I could reach back and cut your head clear off, and in ten minutes I could buy me an alibi that Warren *Burger* couldn't break. I mean, the only way you're ever going to convince a jury to believe an alibi is to bribe eleven of 'em first. Am I right?"

Blixen watched the rain scratch its way along the black windows. "God, I hope not," he said.

CHAPTER FOUR

Merde, That's the Word for Truth

I

The new Hilton (new to Blixen) towered an unexpected twenty-three stories into the sky on a block that in the 1940s had housed a number of retail stores. Across Salmon Street, the marquee of the Broadway Theater advertised an X-rated film. O time, O Broadway, O river endlessly rolling; as a child, Blixen had not been allowed to see *Gone With the Wind* at the Broadway Theater because Clark Gable had said damn in it.

His own X-rated theater had been the raunchy Third Avenue, but after he had registered and been shown to his twenty-second floor suite, the bellman informed him that the Third Avenue had gone through a number of name changes and now housed a respectable company of repertory players. He said that if Blixen cared to see a good show, he could recommend the Jefferson. He said that the films at the Jefferson would make Blixen's hair tremble.

Blixen thanked him, tipped him, and asked him to have room service send up some fried oysters, a bottle of chardonnay, and a box of aspirins. Then he sought out Karen's phone number in the suite's unmutilated directory, dialed it, let it ring eight times, and hung up.

He drowsed on the king-size bed until his dinner arrived. The oysters were sweet, the wine cool. He swallowed three aspirins before eating and three afterward, and by seven-thirty the headache had retreated to a dime-size pulsation behind his left temple.

The rain, meanwhile, had increased. He switched off his bedroom lights and carried the telephone to the window. He asked the operator to get him a Mr. Bernard Lewis at the Kahala Hilton and admired the Willamette bridges twinkling through the downpour until Barney came on the line.

Barney sounded drunk and suspicious. "Hello?"

"Barn, it's Nils."

"Who? Oh, *Nils!* Where the dickens are you! I just got in. Let me switch ears. Are you in Portland?"

"The Hilton, yes. How's Honolulu?"

"Well, Honolulu's just fine!"

"How's Phipps?"

"Hey, he's right here! Why don't you ask him?"

There was a confused rumble at the Kahala end, a fountain of laughter, the thin clink of ice cubes in a glass. Blixen could hear Phipps say querulously: "Who's that, I can't talk now," and then: "Oh."

"Roland?" Blixen said.

"Quick, douse the lights and hide the girls," Phipps boomed. "Here's the producer. Nils, are you keeping your pecker up?"

The jovial, muscular old voice evoked the man. Blixen could see him crouched a bit forward, planted on the balls of his big feet. He would be wearing the Pittsburgh Pirates' baseball hat that Bing had given him. A Hawaiian sports shirt would be stuffed into limp jodhpurs. No director had ever looked more directorial.

"It's pinned right to the top of the mast, Rolly."

"Yipe, pinned. Well, it's your pecker."

"I saw your first day's work."

"Did you enjoy that pan?"

"Absolutely orgasmic."

Phipps chuckled.

"How many reels did you ship today, Rolly?"

"Reels? Who counts? Wait a minute." A hand was clapped over the phone. "Barney? Barney? Barney? How many reels? No, today." The hand was removed. "One," Phipps said.

"One," Blixen repeated.

"If you liked the pan, wait until you see today's work."

"Roland," Blixen said, "aren't you falling a little behind schedule?"

"Am I? I don't know, I never pay any attention to that crap. Like the man says, do you want it good, or do you want it Thursday? I'm not used to this push, push, push. I'm also not used to this spying, if you want to know the truth."

"To—? What spying?"

"First of all, Nils, let me say that I understand the studio's position. They're back there and I'm here and they feel locked out. They want a pipeline to the front, so to speak. Fine. But, Nils, I beg of you, I *beg* of you, the next time you dispatch some lackey all this way to teach the old dog new tricks, will you at least pick somebody that knows his ass from the Grand Canyon?"

"Roland—"

"Hear me out. We're shooting the hotel sequence, right? Working our *butts* off, and up runs this lunatic—"

"Are you talking about Barney Lewis?"

"I'm talking about Barney Lewis, and I mean you really got the prize in the Cracker Jack box when you hired this baby, wow. Here he comes, yelling and screaming and waving his arms. Where's the track, he says, you lost the track, we need the track. On and on—"

"Yes, well, actually," Blixen said, "that was one of my own—"

"Please hear me out, okay? Make a long story short, I says, buddy, did you see the film? He says yes. I says, did you see the flipping trees bent double? Do you have any conception of what a wind of that magnitude does to a sound pick-up? He says, not really. I says, well, it wrecks it, buddy. So we *abandoned* the track, there *is* no track. Make a long story short, he has the gall to check out my mixer, and the mixer says, yeah, we scrubbed the track, we figured we'd loop the whole business. If I were you, I'd fire that dum-dum."

"Don't be absurd."

"Just a suggestion," Phipps said.

"Roland," Blixen said, "about the schedule. You've been on this picture three days and you're already two days behind."

"I'm not proud of it," Phipps said.

"Then don't tell me you never pay attention to scheduling. You promised me three reels a day on location. That's what I expect."

"If you want to jeopardize the quality of this show—"

"I want three reels a day, and the best quality you're capable of giving. I hired Roland Phipps, not some trainee off the streets. Forty years ago you were directing features for Harry Cohn. Do you mean to tell me that Harry Cohn would have accepted two reels for three days' shooting?"

"No, he wouldn't," Phipps said in a low voice.

"How are you going to make up those two lost days?"

"I'm going to work my behind off," Phipps said.

"Who do you love?" Blixen asked.

"I love you, Harry," Phipps said.

Blixen laughed, and said: "I love you, too. Tell Barney I want to talk to him."

"Goodbye, Nils. God bless."

Barney Lewis's voice was awestruck when he returned to the line. "What did you say to him? He patted my rump when he passed."

"I put on my Harry Cohn mask. I think he'll be a good boy now. Forget the two days he's lost. For the kind of film he turns out, I'd let him lose a week. But don't tell him. How's everything else?"

"Well," Barney Lewis began, and then paused. "Never mind, I'll handle it."

"Come on, come on."

"Well, Nils, look," Barney said, "I know Murphy's your star, and I know he's important to the series, but Roland is the least of your problems because what Murphy Smith is doing to this picture is sabotage pure and simple."

"Still crabbing about Rolly's direction?"

"Still crabbing, still calling Todd night and day. He says he's sick. He says if he isn't any better by tomorrow, he'll fly back to Hollywood."

"Where's Murf now?"

"Driving around town somewhere."

"Contact his agent," Blixen said, "and remind him that we have a contractual right to have our own physician check out this mysterious illness. Then get hold of the best internist on Oahu. If Murf refuses to see the doctor, have our legal department declare his contract abrogated."

"And then what?"

"Don't worry about it. He'll see the doctor."

"Suppose he really is sick?"

"Sympathize and shoot around him."

"Boy, I hope you know what you're doing," Barney said. "All right, I'll call you as soon as I see where we stand."

"Thanks, Barn. Good-night."

"Goodbye, Nils."

Blixen replaced the phone on its cradle and stretched out on the bed and listened to the rain lash the windows and stared at the ceiling.

II

Drowsing, he became the central figure in two unrelated dreams. The first was carnal and pleasant.

The second was this nightmare:

He is in a gondola. He is lying on his back in the bottom of the boat. He can hear the red water splashing against the hull beside his ear. There's a word scrawled on the shelf above him. Merde. "Merde," *someone says, "that's the word for truth."*

"Don't be ridiculous," he answers.

"Oh, no, you're the ridiculous one," says the voice.

He strains his head back as far as he is able, and there against the black sky he can discern the outline of the gondolier, who wears a Harlequin costume, yellow and red, and a mask. At first Blixen supposes that the gondolier has drawn a woman's stocking over its head; all the features are mashed down. But then he realizes that there are no features, no eyes, nose, mouth, ears, nothing but skin. The figure leans toward him. "Merde," it whispers, "truth." And it presses its moist blank face against his. Then he understands it all, and he screams and screams and screams. Because the gondolier is Charon. This is the Styx. And he's dead.

III

The scream shook the air.

The shape of the room shivered and steadied, and when the scream recurred, it resolved itself at once into the ring of the telephone.

He rolled onto his side, coughing, knocked the receiver off its hook, and grabbed it. "Yes—"

"Is this the famous TV producer and Professional Boy Wonder, Nils Blixen?"

Blixen consulted his wristwatch. Quarter to eight. "The last time I looked it was," he said. "Who am I speaking to?"

"*Whom* am I speaking to," said the voice. "If you can't be friendly, at least be grammatical."

"Ah," Blixen said, "either I've died and gone to hell, or this is my wretched friend, Gompers."

"Now you *know* hell couldn't be this wet," Gompers cried. "Lucille told me you called, Nils! Can you come down? I'm in the lobby."

"Well, sure, Clem." Blixen ran a hand through his disheveled hair. "Give me five minutes."

"Neat-o," Gompers said.

IV

Downstairs, Gompers was standing by the busy front desk, immersed in a late edition of the *Oregonian*. A second newspaper had been rolled up and stuffed into his raincoat pocket. He had lost and then regained weight and his heavy face was deeply lined; he wore a gray bandit's mustache. Thirty years had turned the plump guinea pig into a potbellied old walrus, myopically digesting the news.

After a moment Blixen strode to the desk. "Clem!"

Gompers wheeled. A second's dismay flashed into and out of his eyes. His right flipper crushed Blixen's, his left gripped Blixen's elbow. "Well, Nils, my goodness!"

"Clemmie, you look exactly the same—"

"So do you!"

"We even lie the same."

Gompers, never swift to adjust, tried a perplexed chuckle.

"Three decades," Blixen said. "That's quite a stretch. But give us time. We'll come into focus."

"You know it," Gompers said vaguely. He continued to pump Blixen's arm. "Say, I love your show. We see it every week. What's the name of it?"

" 'Stagg at Bay.' "

"I thought you did 'Trapper John.' "

"No, 'Stagg at Bay.' "

"Crazy about it," Gompers said. Reluctantly he released Blixen's hand. "Well, Nils, Nils, Nils, the big Hollywood producer. Local boy makes good. Are you married?"

"Divorced."

"I married Lucille," Gompers said. "I ran after her until she caught me." The puzzled look returned to his eyes. "But we've had fun," he went on. "Not that it's been all beer and tickles. You know what I mean. Economically."

"Really?"

"I had a chance to go into my dad's clothing store, but Lucille thought that was a dead end so we started a restaurant. Never cleared a profit. I've had half a dozen businesses since then. Gas station. Hardware. I was even an Avon lady. But I think I'm finally where I want to be. Journalism."

"Terrific, Clem."

"I bought a little West Side sheet." He drew the rolled newspaper out of his pocket and opened it for Blixen. "We hired a typesetter, I'm the editor, Lucille handles circulation."

The paper was called the *Oregon Courier-Chronicle*. Its headline screamed: NEW MEAT MARKET TO OPEN MONDAY!

"We're more or less into local events," Gompers explained. "Here's one we missed, though." He unfolded the other newspaper and tapped a late-news item on the *Oregonian*'s front page. The box was headed: NEW SLASHER VICTIM. "Some kids," he said, "stumbled across a body this afternoon in a house up above Terwilliger. That's where I was headed when Lucille telephoned."

"Is this another derelict murder?" Blixen asked.

"Yeah, another wino bites the dust," Gompers said. "Well, it'll keep Power off our backs for a minute. He's supposed to be in charge of this Slasher business, too. It's too much for one man. But you know Conrad. Stubborn? My God."

"As a matter of fact, I *don't* know Conrad. I wish someone could explain him to me."

"Sure you know him. He went to Grant."

"Power did?"

"He was in our class. Very quiet chap with a nose like a watermelon."

"I don't remember him," Blixen said.

"Well, I didn't either," Gompers confessed, "until I checked the yearbook."

Meditatively Blixen said: "Now, that's funny. I talked to Power for twenty minutes this morning, and he didn't say anything about the Grant connection."

"He doesn't emphasize it. I think he wants to keep a little professional distance there."

Blixen ran his eye again over the brief *Oregonian* story and then handed the paper back. "Clem—I'm supposed to give the police a statement about the night of the party. . . . Would Power be up at this Terwilliger location now, do you think?"

"It's his case, he'd better be."

"And you're on your way there now?"

"Right—"

"Can I come?"

Galvanized, Gompers said: "Hey, neat-o! Sure!"

"The police won't object?"

"How can they? You'll be with a newspaperman. Besides, you're doing research. Trapper John meets the Slasher."

"Stagg."

"I mean Stagg. Go pick up your coat. I'll wait here. I've got a couple of calls to make."

Blixen started toward the elevator bank, hesitated, and circled back. "Oh, Clem—one question before I forget. . . . When you left Coco's party, was Gilbert DeForrest at the house? Do you recall?"

"When I left? Yeah. I was in the kitchen, looking for Lucille, and in DeForrest comes, hopping mad, mad at his *wife* for some reason. He said the mess was all her fault because she couldn't supervise anything. Then he hit her. Terrible. I was afraid he'd clean up on all of us, so the minute he went for the backyard, I lit out. Next thing I remember, I'm at Fifth and Washington, on the Beaumont bus. I walked over to Rich's Cigar Store, looked at the magazines for a while, and then I thought, oh-oh, Lucille, and back I went."

"About what time was this?"

"Oh," Gompers said, "this must have been around midnight, quarter of. The house was lit up like a carnival, but there wasn't a sound, so I went in."

"See anybody else?"

"Not a soul. Then I heard this weak little cry from one of the bedrooms—"

"Lucille," Blixen said.

Gompers blinked.

"She told me she was taking a nap."

"Ah," Gompers said. "Well, I got her on her feet, and we walked down to the Hut. We ended up in Seaside. Flaming youth."

"Lucille said three of you went to Seaside."

"Yeah, Lucille and me and a busboy named Artie Dockweiler. Artie had a car, so when the place closed, away we drove."

"I understand you saw Sophocles."

"In the Hut, yes. Just before we left. Johnny MacVicar came in, too."

"Johnny? Or Mick?"

"Wasn't it Johnny?" Gompers frowned. "I don't know. One or the other. Who can remember after thirty years? That's what I keep telling Power, but you might as well talk to the wall. That is one obstinate cop. I wish they'd never found the damned bones."

"You're not alone," Blixen said.

"Eh?"

"So does the murderer."

CHAPTER FIVE

The Latest Dead Derelict

I

Gompers had parked his battered red Datsun in the hotel garage in a slot marked RESERVED FOR HANDICAPPED, which, Blixen decided, was appropriate in view of the man's crippled driving habits.

Nothing on the car worked. Now and again Gompers would kick the floorboard in an attempt to jar the headlights on, or reach out to flap the broken windshield wiper by hand, but in general they crept forward as blindly as a couple of worms in a cocoon.

Twice they became lost in the soaked hills above Terwilliger Boulevard. As luck would have it, though, Blixen found part of a map under the rubber mat below his feet, and at last they managed to blunder upon the police barricades.

The storm had become a deluge; a waterfall of rain obscured the crime scene. Past the prowl cars, Blixen could make out the smudged lines of a modern wooden house crouched in a thicket of fir and maple.

A black patrolman shone his light over Gompers's face. "No sightseers," he said.

"I'm a reporter," Gompers informed him. *"Courier-Chronicle."*

"Say what?"

"Who's in charge here?" Gompers snapped.

Easily the patrolman replied: "Well, I tell you who ain't, child, and that's you. I never heard of the *Courier-Chronicle*. Go on about your business."

"Do you realize who this gentleman beside me is?"

The flashlight beam stabbed into Blixen's eyes. "Nope," said the patrolman. "Howdy."

"How are you," Blixen replied.

"He's TV," Gompers announced.

The beam steadied. Switched to the rear. "TV? Where's his equipment?"

"Coming," Gompers said.

"Say, Clement," Blixen began, "maybe—"

"I'll handle it," Gompers went on. "So far as I'm aware, there's still a Constitution in this country that guarantees the Four Precious Freedoms and always will, Freedom of the Press, Freedom of TV, Freedom of Radio, Freedom of Access—"

"Freedom to keep out rubberneckers," said the patrolman, but his eyes had grown uncertain.

"Officer," Blixen said, "we understand how busy you all are right now, but if Detective Conrad Power is around, could you just tell him that Nils Blixen from Hollywood is here and wants to talk?"

"Talk about what?"

"The skeleton under the Alameda driveway."

"Believe me, you're going about this all wrong, Nils," Gompers said. "Now if—"

"You keep quiet a minute," said the patrolman. He clasped the flashlight under one arm, hollowed his hands around his mouth, and shouted: "Mr. Power!"

At the top of the drive, a figure turned.

"Man here says he knows something about your Alameda bones! Blitzen!"

"Blixen," Blixen said.

"Blitzen!" the patrolman shouted.

The figure sloshed through the river of water down the drive.

"He be right with you, Mr. Blitzen," said the patrolman.

"Crank your window down, Nils," Gompers said. He sprawled across the seat. "Hey, Connie!" he exclaimed. "Look who I found over at the Hilton—"

A man in a tan raincoat and a soaked tweed cap braced his hands on the lowered window and bent to peer into the car. Conrad Power was in his late forties, somewhat lantern-jawed. His eyes were thoughtful and cavernous, his nose as vast as Durante's. His glance flickered over Gompers, returned to Blixen. "Well,

well," he said. "Mr. Blixen. What a surprise. What happened to Honolulu?"

"I decided to save your people the fuss and the time."

"That's generous, but we could have waited."

"Nils, do you recognize him now?" Gompers asked.

"Not—really," Blixen said, and then, to Power: "I'm told we went to Grant together."

"For about two months," Power said. "I transferred up from Oakland. I never ran around with your group. I didn't remember you kids and I know none of you remembered me. That's why I didn't say anything about it."

"Well, *I* certainly remembered you!" Gompers said and chuckled and patted one of Power's hands.

Power drummed his fingertips against the windowsill and then hunched his shoulders. "I'm drowning," he said. "Move over."

Blixen crowded against Gompers and opened the car door. Power tumbled in, slammed the door shut. "Can this heap make it up the driveway, Mr. Gompers?"

"Like a shot," Gompers said. "And call me Clem."

The Datsun gave five swift explosions and plunged backward into a tangle of blackberry vines. "Whoops!" Gompers cried. "Better check, okay?" He bustled out of the car into the pelting rain.

Power scratched the broad tip of his nose. "I've got a tape recorder up at the house, Mr. Blixen. We'll take your statement there if you don't mind."

"That's why I'm here," said Blixen. "But I warn you, it's not going to help your cause."

"I don't have a cause."

"I'm delighted to hear that."

Power removed his cap and wiped a handkerchief over the back of his neck and looked at Blixen. "What do you think my cause is, exactly?" he asked.

"I hope it's to discover the truth."

"As opposed to what?"

"As opposed to believing that you already know the truth."

"And are you as devoted to that golden concept as you'd like me to be?"

"I think so."

"Yet," Power said, "I somehow arrived at the impression that you're sure Miss Chaplin is innocent."

"I'm—"

"Prejudiced," Power finished. "You've picked your own truth. Like the police. You've examined the evidence, analyzed it, chosen a side. Come to a conclusion. Like the police. What are you doing?"

After a moment, Blixen said: "Prejudging."

"And that's why we need juries, isn't it?"

Blixen watched the rain.

"Do you feel better now?" Power asked.

"Worse."

"Why?"

"Because," Blixen said, "I can't think of anything more dangerous than a sincere, wrong man."

The corners of Power's mouth twitched. "Neither can I, sir," he said.

Blixen considered. "This—evidence you say you've examined against Miss Chaplin—"

"Let's wait for the tape," Power said. "By the way, how did you know where to find me?"

"Gompers figured you'd be investigating the new Slasher killing."

"And who told Gompers there'd been a new Slasher killing?"

"The story's in the *Oregonian*."

"Great," Power said. "And we haven't even removed the body yet. No wonder there've been so many gate-crashers."

"How many derelicts has your man accounted for now?"

"*My* man?"

"I heard that you had a candidate for those murders, too."

Power gave an ambiguous grunt.

"But that you had to release him," Blixen said.

"Harvey Flinders," Power said. "Yeah, we turned him loose this morning."

"To kill again?"

Power jerked his chin toward the house at the top of the drive. "Number five here has been dead about three weeks."

"Which means—what? That number five was killed before you arrested Flinders?"

Power kept his gaze on the house. "Unfortunately," he said, "we arrested Flinders on the seventh of September. He's been in custody ever since."

"Six weeks, more or less."

"More or less."

"Then he's clear so far as this killing goes," Blixen said.

Power said: "Not in my book, he isn't."

"Mr. Power," Blixen said, "if the man was behind bars three weeks ago, he couldn't have committed *this* crime."

"He committed it," Power said.

"How?"

"I don't know yet."

"No possible way you could be wrong?"

"No way."

"I can think of a way," Blixen said. "Why couldn't this be a copycat killing?"

"It couldn't be a copycat killing," Power said, "because copycats can only approximate the legitimate m.o. There are any number of facts we never release. Have you read about the Slasher?"

"Some."

"How does he work?"

"Well," Blixen said, "he attacks drifters, old men. He cuts their genitals off. He quotes the Bible. He leaves a flower behind."

"You've got a very good memory," Power said. "What other organs does he take?"

"I don't know."

"What does he do to the victim's shoes?"

"I don't know."

"How does after-shave lotion enter into it, and what's the brand?"

"I don't know."

"Number five's killer did."

Blixen frowned. "In every instance?"

"Yes, sir."

Presently Blixen said: "So we're faced with three alternatives. Either Flinders figured out a way to kill an old man on Terwilliger Boulevard while he was behind bars in the county jail. Or he had an accomplice who's now going it alone. Or—"

Softly Power murmured: "Or what, sir?"

Blixen raised his eyes. "Or the copycat killer is a cop on the case."

The driver's door burst open. Gompers, streaming water, leaped in, banged the door shut behind him. "Holy cow, men, which way's Ararat? I don't want to fret you boys, but the animals are already pairing up. Are you ready?"

"I thought you were stuck in the mud," Power said.

"What's a little mud to the Fourth Estate?" Gompers asked. "Fasten your seat belts."

This time they made it.

II

"Swinnerton!" Power shouted. "Swinnerton!"

He slammed the front door behind them and wiped his feet on a Persian hall runner. He slapped the water off his cap, pointed toward the living room. "Go on in and sit down someplace. I'll be back in a second."

A door at the end of the hallway opened and a policewoman in a green parka thrust her head around it. "Oh, it's you," she said.

"Swinnerton, who's supposed to be on this door?" Power barked. "Half of Portland could have tramped in and out of here by now."

"Don't look at me. Somebody says watch the door, somebody else says make the coffee, I haven't got six hands." Swinnerton was broad-hipped and big-bosomed, built low to the ground, like a wartime pillbox. Her discontented eyes had a Tartar slant. She spoke in a smoker's baritone and every word she uttered seemed to scare the bejesus out of Gompers. "Want some Sanka?" she asked.

"I'll get it," Power said. "Come here."

Her tread shook the house.

"New job for you, baby-sitting," Power went on. "Stay with these two gentlemen for a couple of minutes. Have they dug the victim out yet?"

"Huh-uh, still at it," Swinnerton answered.

Nodding, Power disappeared down the hall.

Swinnerton motioned. "In there, boys. Watch your step."

Lights blazed in the sunken living room. In the cellar, a gas furnace wheezed and labored, but seemed to send up very little heat. The sweet smell of corruption tainted the air. Blixen found a register to stand over, and breathed through his mouth.

Avidly Gompers prowled past a pile of pillows. He had pulled a sodden notebook out of his shirt pocket and was trying to separate the leaves. "Power asked you if they'd dug him out yet. Dug him out of what?"

"Bomb shelter or a fruit cupboard or some grotesque thing hacked out of the earth at the west end of the cellar," Swinnerton said. "There's a judas hole, but the door's locked."

"You're pulling my leg. Seven hundred specialists running around here and not one of them can open a *fruit* cupboard?"

"I offered to pick the lock with a hairpin, but who listens to us silly-billy girl cops?"

"Why don't you get a key from the owners?" Blixen asked.

"We can't contact the owners. The neighbor says they're in Mexico. We had to bust a window to get in. Then we found another one busted in the back."

"Is that who reported the murder?" Gompers asked. "This neighbor?" He had given up on his pulpy notebook. He bent a matchbook cover back to scribble on.

"No, a kid's dog came sniffing around, started barking, the kid smelled something funny—"

"And how much of the fruit cupboard can you make out through the judas hole?"

"Too much," Swinnerton said.

"You've seen the body?"

"Sure."

"Describe it."

"What are you, a ghoul?"

"Oh, come on," Gompers said, "I've been briefed. I'm not going to print it. I just—"

"*Print* it?" Swinnerton interrupted. She gawked at Blixen.

"He's a newspaperman," Blixen explained.

In the rear, a door crashed twice against a wall. "Swinnerton!" Power shouted thinly.

Empurpled, Swinnerton strode to the hall archway. "What!"

"Come on down, we need you!"

"I thought you told us to keep the press out!" Swinnerton bellowed.

"Never mind all that, come here!"

Swinnerton pointed at Gompers. "*You* I'll attend to later." Arms swinging, she charged down the hall.

Gompers had broken into a sweat. "Gracious little creature," he said.

"Don't let her intimidate you, Clement. Remind her of the Four Precious Freedoms."

"Who's intimidated?"

Footsteps pounded toward the entryway, and Gompers was off like a shot for the front door. But it was only Power. "Excuse me," Power said, and then hauled the door open and bawled: "Somebody bring a stretcher!" He muttered: "Gangway," and ran back to hold the swinging kitchen door for two male cops who were lugging a canvas dead-sack between them. A gray-haired man in civilian clothes followed, stripping off a pair of elbow-length surgical gloves. Swinnerton trailed the civilian with an armload of clear plastic evidence bags. Over the handkerchief pressed to his nose, Blixen could make out a handful of crackers, three undistinguished Irish potatoes, a couple of crushed cans of dog food, a soiled bandanna, a wilted black pansy.

"Same m.o., Doctor?" Gompers asked.

"No comment," said the gray-haired man.

"Biblical reference on the wall?"

"You heard him, no comment," Power repeated, and beckoned two dripping ambulance attendants forward. The object in the dead-sack, loose and obscene, was transferred to the stretcher. Blixen tightened the handkerchief against his nose and looked away while the attendants and the doctor trotted out.

"Everybody through here?" Power asked. "Seal it up. Oh." He tapped Blixen's shoulder. "About that statement—"

Tentatively Blixen lowered the handkerchief. The odor was distinct but bearable. "Why don't I come in Monday."

"What's your local address again?"

"The Hilton."

Power reflected. "I could drop you off. We could talk on the way."

"Personally, Nils," Gompers warned, "I'd want a lawyer present. He's entitled to representation, Power."

"I'll see you Monday," Power said and turned.

But Blixen stopped him. "Thanks. I'll accept the lift."

"There goes the Fifth Precious Freedom," Gompers said.

CHAPTER SIX

Two Halves of One
Cardboard Figure

I

"How do you feel about tape recorders?" Power asked.

"They inhibit me."

"Here," Power said. He rapped his knuckles against Blixen's knee and held out a flat silver and black instrument the size of a cigarette case.

They had slipped down the drive in Power's Granada onto a private road that corkscrewed through unkempt woods. The night was deafening; it was impossible to see ten feet into the ocean of rain. Blixen indicated the case. "What's this?"

"The recorder. Take it."

"Why?"

"For reassurance. The control button's on the lower left. When you're ready to make a statement, switch it on. If you want to talk off the record, kill it."

Blixen contemplated the machine, shifted the button. A bell rang.

"Oh-oh," Power said. "She's run out. Well, so much for tape recorders."

"Uh-huh," Blixen said. "You know, if this were TV, the wily cop would have a second secret tape rolling somewhere."

"That's why you guys make the big money," Power said. "I never would have thought of that."

"Where is it?" Blixen asked.

"Glove compartment," Power said.

Blixen lowered the compartment door. Reels hissed in a topless box.

"Now you won't respect me anymore," Power said. "I suppose you prefer it off."

"Please."

Power touched a switch on his dash and the reels sighed to a stop.

"Thank you."

"You'll just have to come in Monday and do it all over again."

"I'll be there," Blixen said. "Me and my attorney."

Power grimaced and settled deeper into his bucket seat.

"Meanwhile," Blixen said, "I don't see why two former class-mates couldn't have a casual, off-the-record, unwitnessed conver-sation about old times."

"Sure you don't want to check the rest of the car out first?" Power asked. "What if I've hidden a dwarf under the lap robe and he's taking all this down in shorthand?"

"You're wily, but you aren't *that* wily," Blixen said.

They had reached Terwilliger Boulevard. Across from them the Hillvilla restaurant gleamed through the rain. After a dyspeptic moment, Power turned left toward town. "Waste of time, but what the hell," he said. "Okay, off the record—why did you leave Port-land so soon after the graduation party?"

"I went to California."

"I understand that. I'm not asking you where you went. I'm asking why you went."

"What difference does it make?"

Power shot him a curious glance. "Well, let's examine it. You save the girl of your dreams from a rapist, you romance her for eight or ten solid hours, you stagger off at the dawn's early light and you promptly set out for California. Furthermore, you never try to see or contact the woman again. Is that the act of your aver-age lovesick adolescent?"

There was no heater in the car. A chill lay on Blixen's bones. "Not the way you tell it," he said.

"Fine. *You* tell it."

"I'd intended to leave for weeks—"

Wildly Power kicked at his brake, spun the wheel. An R.V. had lumbered off the shoulder onto the road ahead of them. Tires shrieked—

The whole world tilts, reeling. Karen shoves him aside and marches out of the garden into the house, dress torn, head erect. Sophocles has vanished. Coco is nowhere to be seen. Blixen drags himself into the gazebo, cracks one of the beer bottles and drinks and drinks. He has lost all sense of time. Only when something rouses him does he realize that he has drifted off. He is sprawled on the gazebo sofa and the moon seems to be in an entirely different section of the sky and Coco is weeping in the distance and just as Blixen hauls himself out of the gazebo, here comes Gilbert DeForrest through the kitchen door like a bull elephant, trumpeting and terrible. DeForrest resembles the Victorian's idea of a Bedlamite. His eyes bulge, his lips froth. He asserts that his lawn and garden are wrecked beyond repair, and he demands restitution. He'll have the police on them all. Blixen leaves him weeping for his broken flowers, and slips into the house where Mrs. DeForrest, for some mad reason, has seated herself on the floor between the bread bin and the refrigerator, and is nursing a bruised lip. Blixen calls for Karen, but receives no answer. He staggers outside, stumbles down the front lawn. There is no sign of Karen or anyone else. He heads across the dark T-intersection and up the street to the Chaplin house. The Chaplin driveway is pitch-black. He thinks he can see someone running toward the rear. He bounds forward and slams into a form that materializes before him. MacVicar screams—

Screeching, Power's Granada danced along the road's shoulder, regained the asphalt, shuddered, steadied.

Up ahead, the van's taillight disappeared. Power's lips were white. "Son of a gun," he rasped. "Are you hurt? I'll stop by the medical school. You've hit your head."

"It's nothing, forget it." Blixen wadded his rain-soaked handkerchief into a ball and dabbed it against the wound.

Fretfully, Power said: "There's insurance—"

"I'll tell you what you *can* do for me," Blixen said. He examined the watery red handkerchief. "Drop me off at Broadway Drive. There's someone I want to see. I'll call a cab."

"In this rain? You'd never find one. Where do you want to go?"

"John MacVicar's house, Portland Heights."

"I know where it is. I'll take you."

The two lapsed into silence. Blixen tapped at his clotted wound and restarted the bleeding. Irritated, he plastered the handkerchief against his forehead.

In a vacant tone, Power said: "What were we talking about? Oh. Your sudden flight. You were telling it your way. Go ahead."

Blixen hesitated. "That's it. It's a little vague to me now. It was a long time ago. I wanted Karen to come with me, but—she may have been afraid to just—cut out like that."

"Afraid the contractors would find the body she'd buried, perhaps," Power said, "and wonder about her precipitous flight."

"Mr. Power," Blixen murmured, "what's your rating?"

"I'm a sergeant."

"Which means that you've amassed a good deal of experience."

"Some."

"Enough, at any rate, to know for sure that any jury born of woman would laugh your case against Karen Chaplin out of court. In fact you don't have a case. Why are you doing this?"

"In fact you don't know what I have," Power said.

They had turned left off 6th Avenue. They stopped for a red light at Broadway.

"You're peering at me," Power said.

"You mean," said Blixen, "that there's more?"

"More? Certainly there's more."

"Like what?"

"Come now. Does Macy's tell Gimbels?" The green light appeared. They veered left, toward a bridge and Broadway Drive and the hills. "Just take my word for it," Power said comfortably. "We've got your lady up a tree, and we've got the axes to bring her down. She hated Sophocles Kanaris. She stabbed him. And I think you know it."

"All over but the shouting," Blixen said.

"All virtually over."

"And yet every single soul at that party hated Sophocles enough to kill him."

"Including you?"

"Of course. He tried to rape my girl."

"As a result of which," Power said, "you crept out of your

girl's bed later that evening, you snuck back to the DeForrest house, you stripped Sophocles naked, and you stabbed him."

"I stripped him *naked?*"

"He was certainly naked when he was buried," Power said.

"How do you know that?"

"There were no clothes in the grave."

"Well, *would* there have been? Wouldn't they have rotted in thirty years?"

"Buttons wouldn't. Zippers wouldn't. The blade of the butcher knife that killed him didn't."

Blixen folded his handkerchief, stuffed it into his jacket pocket.

Power craned an eye at Blixen over his beak. "Conjures up a curious picture, doesn't it? Now what do you suppose that ugly Greek gardener was doing out there in the buff?"

"Maybe he was worshiping the moon."

"Yes," Power conceded, "maybe. Or maybe an attractive girl convinced him that she wanted to play around a little more. So that she could disarm him, and take him by surprise."

"You," Blixen said, "have got to be kidding."

Power smiled. "All right, I'm kidding."

"But even if you aren't," Blixen went on, "why limit your suspects? Sophocles would have stripped for anything, including the beasts of the field. How can you eliminate any of us? Coco, Gilbert DeForrest. What about DeForrest, by the way?"

"What about him?"

"He disappeared the day after the murder. Do you know why?"

"Family troubles. And he didn't disappear. He went to Chicago. He died there in nineteen fifty-three. Cancer. He'd developed a sarcoma."

"Suppose he'd also developed a guilty conscience?"

"He probably had. But not for murdering Sophocles."

"You can't be sure of that."

"Yes, I can," Power said. "Because I know who did murder him."

II

By the time they'd reached Davenport Street, snow crystals had begun to appear between the fat raindrops. As they rounded the curve, Power broke his long silence. "Is MacVicar expecting you?"

"No."

"Then you aren't even sure he's home. I'll wait until you're inside."

He eased to a stop below a bank half smothered in azaleas and Japanese maple. A broad-beamed white Victorian house perched on the top of a hillock.

"I see lights," Blixen said. "He's home."

"I'll wait."

"You never give up, do you?"

"Never give up."

A smile played over Blixen's mouth. "Sergeant," he said, "that makes two of us." He shoved the door open and galloped up a mossy path under a canopy of waterlogged branches that whacked and hissed against his topcoat. MacVicar had painted his staid doorway a raffish turquoise. A bell handle stuck out of the wall under a plaque that said, in a copperplate hand: "Ring me." And who'll answer, Blixen wondered, the Red Queen?

He yanked the handle and thought he heard a gong boom in the bowels of the house.

A peephole opened. The face behind the grille was indistinct. "John?" Blixen said.

"I don't know you," the man answered. "What do you want?"

"I'm looking for Dr. MacVicar. Tell him it's a friend. The name is Blixen. I should have phoned, but—"

"Are you *Nils?*" MacVicar broke in. "You *are* Nils! Where did you—! I've—! All right." A chain clanked. The door strained and shook. "Wait a minute—"

Blixen touched his thumb to his finger in an "okay" sign to Power, but Power maintained his vigil until the door had opened and MacVicar had drawn Blixen inside. Then he honked twice in farewell and sped away.

MacVicar half opened the door again and scowled out.

"That was Sergeant Power," Blixen explained. "We've been having a talk. He drove me over."

MacVicar closed the door, lost.

Voices murmured out of a room at the end of the hall. Blixen said: "John—listen—if you're busy—"

"No, no, I'm not!" MacVicar cried. "I was just watching TV—rotting my brain, eh?" The hand around Blixen's upper arm shook almost imperceptibly. "But how long have you been in town? The Gomperses were over last month and Clem said you were living in California—"

"I was. I am. I flew up this afternoon—"

"This—oh! To give a statement? Yes, they've been after all of us about that skeleton." MacVicar wore a khaki leisure suit and a ginger beard. He was thinner than Blixen remembered, more urbane, somehow less bucktoothed. His eyes seemed feverish. He pounced at Blixen's shoulders. "Here, let me take your coat. I'm not thinking. The doctor gave me some pain pills. And I had a drink, like an idiot. Go on in. I'll turn the TV off."

He threw Blixen's coat over a bench and strode down the hall. Blixen followed a crackling sound into a warm ivory-colored living room. A huge blaze sizzled in the fireplace. Books stood in perilous towers on cabinets and end tables. A harpsichord shrank against one wall under a copy of the Decker portrait of W. C. Fields as Queen Victoria. The rugs on the polished hardwood floor were American Indian.

"Would *you* like a drink?" MacVicar called. "All I've got is gin."

"Gin's fine."

A paperback novel lay open on a leather chair. *Le Avventure d'Alice nel Paese delle Meraviglie*. Blixen held his hands to the fire, turned at the sound of footsteps and accepted a jelly glass from MacVicar.

"Salud," MacVicar said and drank out of his own jelly glass. "Sit down, Nils! Just toss the book on the floor."

"An Italian Alice? I didn't realize you knew Italian."

"Poco, poco. I flounder along. You might say I speak a little Verdi."

"Like Mick."

MacVicar glanced at him and drank again.

"Mick spoke Italian," Blixen said. "Or always claimed he did."

"You've got us confused," MacVicar said. "Mick could barely speak *English.* I was the language student." He stared at the fire. "You heard Mick died—"

"Lucille told me. I'm sorry."

"That bloody war!" MacVicar hurled his drink over the fire screen onto the glowing grate. The explosion spewed glass and sparks up the chimney and across the Indian rug. Blixen stamped wildly on the coals. "Oh, let it go," MacVicar muttered in a cranky undertone. "The housekeeper'll be here Monday. She'll straighten things up."

"You don't want the place to burn down—!"

"Why don't I?"

Unsettled, Blixen continued to kick at the rug. "John, do you feel all right? Can I get you something?"

"Just Mickey." Red veins glistened in MacVicar's eyes. "Don't ever be born a twin, Nils," he said. "It isn't worth the pain. Let go. What are you doing?"

"It's late and you're tired. Where's the bedroom?"

"Let go, let go," MacVicar said. He tugged out of Blixen's grip, sprawled onto the sofa. "Just give me a second. It's the codeine. My whole head hurts. Never drink and drive. Or—that's not it. Never drink and—"

"And take pills."

"And take pills, exactly. But I had so much to think about. I was so surprised when I walked in. I still can't imagine what it means, can you? Well, I'll check it out tomorrow." MacVicar braced his elbows on his knees and rested his chin in the Y made by the heels of his hands. The fire spat and pulsated. Slowly MacVicar's lids sagged, snapped up again. "So, Nils," he boomed, "you're back! The prodigal returns. How does Portland look to you? Have you seen Karen?"

"Not yet."

"Karen's—" MacVicar began, and hesitated. "I suppose Power filled you in—about the murder—"

"He hit the high points."

"Karen's a suspect."

"Yes, he told me." Blixen leafed through the Italian Alice. "And that's asinine. We'll just have to uncover the truth ourselves and rub his nose in it."

There was no answer. Blixen closed the paperback, placed it on an end table, watching MacVicar.

At last MacVicar lifted his head. It swayed lethargically on its stem, like an old flower in a November gust. "I'm sorry. What?"

"I say it's asinine to think that Karen could have killed anyone."

"Oh."

"Or—is she a suspect in your mind, too?"

"Nils," MacVicar said, "I'm a psychiatrist. There's no one on earth I'd put murder past."

"Given motive, you mean, and opportunity."

"Given motive in particular. Motive," MacVicar said, and massaged his enflamed eyes, "motive is the fulcrum of crime, the essence. Once I was asked to examine a twelve-year-old girl who was suspected of having locked her grandfather in a bedroom and set the house on fire. But there was no motive, the police said. Well, I talked to the girl. I found her vain and timid and much younger than her years. I tried complimenting her on her poise. Within minutes she'd confessed to me that the old man had criticized the color of her nail polish. He'd said it was too old for her. So she'd burnt him to death." The account seemed to have invigorated MacVicar. He gave a short bark of a laugh. "Motive," he said.

Thoughtfully Blixen said: "You say the police asked you to examine this child—"

"Well, the court asked me."

"Do you often do this kind of work?"

"Not often. Now and again."

"Ever work specifically with Conrad Power?"

"We've—had some contact, yes."

"What do you think of him?"

"Competent. Not too bright. Stubborn."

"Capable of murder?"

MacVicar, reaching toward a cigarette box, arrested his hand. "I told you. Anyone's capable of murder."

Blixen turned back to the fire. "John, Power indicated to me that he had a much stronger case against Karen than he was telling. Do you know anything about that?"

After a moment MacVicar said: "He's told me the same thing."

"Has he ever asked your psychiatric opinion of Karen?"

"I have no psychiatric opinion of Karen," MacVicar said. "Karen's never been a patient of mine."

"Yet you wouldn't agree when I suggested that Power was coming down too hard on her."

No answer.

"*Do* you think she killed Sophocles?"

"Yes," MacVicar said.

Blixen drew a poker out of the fire set on the hearth and dug in a desultory way at the powdery side of the logs. "May I ask why?"

"If you want. But I won't tell you."

"Surely it can't be privileged information."

"Not legally, no. On the other hand, it's confidential."

After a last punch at the disintegrating logs, Blixen returned the poker to its stand. "All right, let me ask you about the night of the party. Did you see the fracas between Karen and Sophocles?"

"I missed that. Mick and I were in the kitchen. We heard you yelling, and then Karen came rushing in. There was a butcher knife on the table. She grabbed it and threatened to kill Sophocles. But Mrs. DeForrest wrestled the knife away from her and Karen ran out. So Mick and I beat it, too."

"Together?"

"We were always together. We were two halves of one cardboard figure, Nils." Once more MacVicar reached for the cigarette box. He dislodged the box's lid, sent it clattering onto the floor. "That's why it hurt so bad when we were pulled apart."

Blixen said: "And where did you go after you left the party?"

"Where? I can't remember. We walked around."

"Did you see Karen?"

"No."

"I thought you might have been looking for her," Blixen said, "when I ran into you on the Chaplin driveway."

The old house bent against the storm; wind whispered down the chimney. MacVicar apparently noticed the cigarette in his hand for the first time. "Look at this," he said. "What am I doing? I haven't smoked for six months." He ground the cigarette out and lit another and held it between his ring and little finger and rubbed his thumb across his right eyebrow, eyes closed.

"I left after DeForrest came home," Blixen persisted. "I decided to drop by Karen's. I headed up her driveway—and I bumped into someone. Was that you?"

"No."

"Then it was Mick. He screamed. Someone else ran toward the backyard. Was *that* you?"

"No."

"Do you know who it was?"

Wearily MacVicar said: "Oh, Nils, let it go. It didn't have anything to do with you or the murder."

"Why did Mick scream like that?"

Back and forth went the thumb over the eyebrow. At last MacVicar said: "You startled him."

"Who ran into the backyard?"

"Sophocles."

"*Sophocles* was outside the Chaplin house?"

"Sophocles," MacVicar said, "was *in* the Chaplin house. He came out of that side door on the driveway just as we walked past. So Mick went over. But a couple of minutes later, you barged up and everybody split."

Lightning sparkled against the wide front window. Thunder stumbled and crumped. MacVicar bent forward to toss his cigarette away. Fire shine smeared his leisure jacket. "I asked you to let it go, Nils," he said.

Linking his hands behind him, Blixen walked to the harpsichord. A narrow tube lamp cast a harsh light on a book of hymns propped against the rack. "Sophocles was in the house," he said.

"In it, yes."

"Karen was home by then. Are you claiming she'd invited Sophocles over?"

"I'm not claiming anything. I'm telling you what I saw."

"Did you see Karen?"

"No."

"Did Sophocles make any reference to her?"

"No."

Blixen set his fingers on the cool harpsichord keys, played the first delicate, incongruous notes of "Onward, Christian Soldiers."

"Nils," MacVicar said, "there's a theory that the body goes through a complete change every seven years. That the atoms reform, and that we literally become different people."

"What's your point?"

"Well, I wonder," MacVicar said, "if you might not be trying to defend a girl who no longer exists." He coughed, and then found a handkerchief and coughed into that. "Or who never existed."

"The girl I knew existed," Blixen said. "And she could not have committed a murder."

"And you'll march blindly into hell," MacVicar said, "defending her."

"I don't believe I'm in the least blind."

"And what do you believe Don Quixote was when he attacked the windmills?"

"Wrong."

"And bull-headed," MacVicar said. "And blind." He brooded. "You see, Nils," he said, "the hard thing isn't the attack on the mirage. It's recognizing that your lady's the village slut." At once he raised his hand. "I withdraw 'slut,'" he said. "That was uncalled for."

After a time Blixen said: "Let's go back. When I came along, you all split. Why?"

Curiously MacVicar said: "You really do want to hear it all, don't you?" He shrugged. "All right. Sophocles was selling. Mick was buying. You wouldn't have approved."

"So Sophocles sold Mick a couple of dirty pictures. What's—"

"Not pictures. Dirty veins."

Mishearing, Blixen said: "Dirty—?"

"Veins," MacVicar repeated. "Veins, veins, V-E-I-N-S."

Still off-balance, Blixen said: "But—are you implying—? What are you implying? Hard drugs?"

"Of course."

"Sophocles pushed—" Blixen's head continued to reel. "Who else was on this stuff?"

"Half the neighborhood."

"I don't believe it."

"Don't, it's all the same to me."

"Karen?"

"I don't know."

"Gompers?"

"I think so."

"He never showed it."

"Maybe he was never hooked."

"Was Mick?"

"Clear up to his ears."

"But the Army wouldn't have drafted an addict—"

"He kicked it."

"When?"

MacVicar stared into the flames. "We left town that night. The night of the party. I drove him over to central Oregon. Where he could yell to his heart's content. Took him ten mortal days."

Blixen lowered himself to the harpsichord bench. "Well, I'm damned," he said.

"I don't have to tell you he was back on it before he was through basic," MacVicar said. "Speaking of damnation."

Blixen groped toward another thought. "I interrupted the sale, then—"

"Only until we could catch up to the source."

"At the Hut?"

Surprised, MacVicar said: "Yes. How did you know that?"

"Who made the buy? You?"

"I wouldn't touch the stuff. Mick did his own buying."

"In the restaurant?"

"No, he was shaking all over by then. We spotted Gompers and Lucille at the counter. Mick didn't want them to see him. He had me call Sophocles outside. We got Mick fixed up, and drove around for a while, and that was that."

"Did you notice the time?"

"It was after midnight. We dropped Sophocles off at about twenty minutes to one."

"Dropped him where?"

"A block and a half from Karen's place," MacVicar said.

Presently Blixen said: "Have you told this story to Power?"

"I have."

"And he believes it?"

"He does."

"Why?"

"Just before Sophocles left us, we were speeding down Fremont," MacVicar murmured. "Prowl car stopped us at Thirty-eighth. The officer thought we looked suspicious, so he took our names and addresses and ran a stolen-car check. The car was clean, of course. The officer's notes indicate that Sophocles Kanaris walked back toward Forty-first to catch a late bus, and that John MacVicar, driver, and Michael MacVicar, passenger, proceeded west on Fremont and then south on Thirty-third. He followed us all the way to Sandy. Just to make sure we remained good boys. It's all in the record."

The wind had risen. Threads of bluish smoke from the blocked chimney puffed into the room. MacVicar dredged the handkerchief out of his hip pocket again and flapped it at the fireplace.

But Blixen scarcely notices him. Reeky and acrid, the smoke buzzes in his nose. MacVicar, after the shriek, has hightailed it off the Chaplin driveway and up the street. Karen has materialized on the front porch. She stands in the red doorway in a white, quilted, girlish robe strewn with tiny bluebirds. But surely she is nude beneath it. "Who was that? Who yelled?" she asks, and he tells her MacVicar, though he doesn't know which one. Or care, at this point. Anticipation has made him sad and sick. Behind Karen the fire blazes. She stands aside and he enters the hazy strange room. She divines his queasy looks around. "Mom and Dad are away," she says. "They won't be back." The robe slips from her shoulders. She sits on a pillow in front of the fire, her chin on her bare knees, her arms hugging her calves. Blixen has never seen a live naked female before. Nothing has ever seemed to him so defenseless, more tender. He sinks to his knees beside her. Her face is in shadow, featureless, masked. He whispers: "Karen . . ."

And then, in astonishment: "Charon?"

MacVicar rotated his head. "What?"

"That was the gondolier—"

MacVicar fanned the smoke away from his face and sat back on his haunches.

Confused, Blixen met his eyes. "I had a dream this afternoon," he said. "It shook me—and I don't know why. Except that it involved death."

"Oh, *that* Charon," MacVicar grunted. "What sort of a dream?"

Lightning darted over the soused windowpane, thunder reverberated. "Well, I was dead," Blixen resumed slowly. "Charon was rowing me. We were in the Styx, in a gondola. I could hear the red river outside. I couldn't see it, but I knew it was the color of blood. Somebody had written *merde* on the coffin top above my head. The gondolier told me that was the word for truth."

"You were in Italy, you think?"

"Yes, on the river Po." Blixen drew his brows together. "Does that make sense? Is the Po in Venice?"

"South of Venice," MacVicar said absently.

"Bad geography."

MacVicar squeezed his long hands together. "Nils, I'm going to suggest three words to you. You supply the next one, the first thing that pops into your head. Death. Red. Mask."

"Poe," Blixen answered. For a moment he remained immobile. Then he lifted his hands, let them fall against his legs.

"Don't scorn puns, my friend," MacVicar told him. "Puns allow the subconscious to pick up pain and look at it. Something's bugging you. Something you can't remember—or you won't remember. Poe. Masque of the Red Death. Charon. In the Styx—"

"On the Styx."

"You said in. You're a Los Angeleno now. How do you think of Portland? I mean, as to size?"

"It's compact, it's pretty. I'm not sure I could live way up here in the boondocks—"

"And what's another word for boondocks?"

The wind had changed. Over the grate, the wavering smoke ascended straight up the chimney again. Blixen studied the play of the firelight on the ceiling.

"Don't turn away from it, Nils," MacVicar said. "Here you are, dead in the sticks. Now, what do you suppose you're trying to tell yourself?"

"To stay away from fried oysters in October."

"You say you were lying in a kind of coffin. So was Sophocles."

When Blixen sought MacVicar's face, MacVicar leaned away from the light. "Are you warm enough? Your eyes seem tired. Close them."

"Quit it. It won't work. I can't be hypnotized."

"Because you're a very controlled person, and you're afraid you'll lose control. But hypnotism isn't a bludgeon behind the ear. It's an agreement to cooperate, quiet times, a stroll with a friend, a buoyant float on a summer lake, the bluest sky, the slowest clouds."

"I warn you, I'm aware of everything that's happening."

"More than that—you're aware of what happened before. No more barriers. No more fighting. You've stumbled over a kind of coffin, a grave. But it isn't in a gondola. Where is it?"

"Backyard."

"Whose backyard?"

"DeForrest's."

"Describe it for me."

"Everybody's gone. It's late. There's a ditch along the side of the house. For a new driveway. I walk toward the ditch—"

"Look at the ditch. Tell me what you see."

"Nothing."

"What's in the ditch, Nils? There's something there that you can't face. Look at it."

"*Merde,*" Blixen said.

"Is that the word for truth?"

"*Merde.*"

"Your accent's changing. Say it again."

"*Mord.*"

"And what does *Mord* mean?"

"I don't know."

"Yes, you do. We both took German in school. What does *Mord* mean?"

"Murder," Blixen said, and pressed his thumbs into his eyes until color flamed there like fireworks in a July sky.

"Did you see the murder, Nils?"

Greens, electric blues, pinwheels, and MacVicar's insistent voice miles and miles away. "Nils, who did you see? Who's standing by the driveway? Look at the face."

The voice is lost in the roaring. There is no face. The colors spring and burst across the stage of his mind like fountains playing, stars shooting. They leap and dazzle and dance. And if there are actors present somewhere, they are altogether hidden now behind this crazy curtain.

III

"The rain's stopped," Blixen said.

Through the double-paned kitchen window he could make out a

rhododendron bush spread against the wind. MacVicar had heated a pan of water, and was stirring instant Yuban into a couple of cups.

"Cream?" MacVicar asked. "Sugar?"

"Cream, please."

They resembled visiting mandarins in their exquisite mutual deference. MacVicar set a cup and a cream pitcher on the table. His feverish air had been replaced by a sort of heartbroken regret, as if he had counted enormously on Blixen and had been enormously disappointed. He sipped at his coffee. "How do you feel?"

"I'm all right."

"Nils," MacVicar said, and lowered the cup and wiped the back of a forefinger over his mouth, "I do hope you realize I was trying to help? I mean, what do I care who killed the man or why? I'm not on Power's side. If I'm on anybody's side, it's Karen's. I simply wanted to help you break through to the truth. Which you did. Now we understand why you rushed off to California."

Blixen continued to stir his coffee. He'd poured too much cream into it; it had taken on an alabaster tone, the alien sheen of taffy soup.

"I mean, obviously," MacVicar continued, "you weren't about to turn your girl friend in for murder. Nobody's going to blame you for that."

"Isn't it interesting," Blixen murmured, "how sure you are that it was Karen I saw."

"Wasn't it?"

Was it? *At the edge of the ravaged driveway, a figure stirs smokily. A shovel has just been plunged into the soft earth. In the grave itself, Sophocles, evidently having died guffawing, wears a rictus on his ashen mouth.*

"I saw Sophocles in the grave," Blixen said. "I saw someone above him—"

"Karen."

"I can't tell."

MacVicar's glaze of Chinese courtesy had begun to crack. "Well, Nils, who else could it have been? You discovered your love in a pickle and you ran! Perfectly natural sequence of—"

In a dogged undertone, Blixen said: "I don't think it was Karen."

"But if—!" Abruptly MacVicar stretched his neck in its loose sport-shirt collar, and tried a ringing, careless laugh. "Well, well," he said. "All right, Quixote, you have it your way."

"I'm not out to have it my way," Blixen protested. "If I saw Karen over that grave, she must have seen me. In that case, why in heaven's name would she call on me for an alibi?"

"She called on Quixote." MacVicar jackknifed forward. "Nils, the woman knows you better than you know yourself! But I tell you something, my friend, she's running one hell of a risk. And so are you. Because, how does Quixote react when he finally accepts the truth?"

"For a psychiatrist—"

"He reacts," MacVicar interrupted, "he *reacts* the same way Sam Spade did! He admits his mistake. He turns the lady in, no matter what it costs him, and even if he has somehow convinced himself that he could never do that!" Panting, MacVicar smoothed down the thin hair on the top of his head, and stretched his neck again and said: "Boy, I wouldn't be in your shoes for all the nuts in Brazil. What's the matter with your coffee?"

Distracted, Blixen said: "Nothing—it's good—"

"You aren't drinking it."

"The rain's back," Blixen said. "Listen."

"You're in Oregon. What did you expect? Ignore it."

"I can't ignore it, I've got to get out in it," Blixen said. "I'd better call a cab, John. Where's your phone?"

"Grand, I've wounded you," MacVicar said.

"You haven't wounded me. It's been a long day and I'm beat." Blixen indicated a plastic figure of Snoopy beside a breadbox. "Is *that* the phone?"

"Will you cool it? Please? I'll drive you myself!" Morosely MacVicar hoisted himself to his feet and dug his hands into both front pants pockets. "Keys . . ." Suddenly his eyes crossed. He freed his right hand and delivered a slap to the center of his forehead. "I *won't* drive you!" he said. "My transmission's out!"

"There you go," Blixen said. "Now how do I dial this dog?"

"Will you kindly get *away* from there?" MacVicar yanked the phone out of his hand. "At least I can be host enough to call for you. Bathroom's down the hall—first door on the left. Where are you staying?"

"Hilton."

"Hilton," MacVicar muttered, and began dialing.

IV

In the chilly bathroom, Blixen relieved himself, found a sliver of
soap on the bottom shelf of the medicine cabinet, and washed his
hands. There was a framed piece of sheet music over the toilet.
The cover depicted a drab old lady in a rocker. The song was entitled "Granny, You're My Mammy's Mammy," and it was by the
authors of "My Mammy," Joe Young and Sam M. Lewis, and
Harry Akst. It made Blixen feel better. Calmed, he returned to the
empty kitchen, and then proceeded on into the living room, where
MacVicar sat peeling an apple.

MacVicar looked up and said: "Well, we're screwed again. I
called both cab companies and they laughed in my face. There'll
be at least an hour's wait." He munched moodily. "I'd invite you
to stay here," he said, "except that I'm not really set up for it."

"John, don't worry, I'll be fine," Blixen said.

"Or you could take the bus," said MacVicar.

Blixen said: "I'll take the bus."

"The shelter's right across the street. Buses come on the half
hour. You've got three minutes."

Electrified, Blixen said: "And where did you say this shelter
is?"

"I'll show you."

They strode into the entryway. While Blixen struggled into his
coat, MacVicar cracked the front door open. "See there? By the
little drinking fountain. Your bus will be number Fifty-one. Coun-
cil Crest. You can stay if you want, you know. I could make up a
cot in the cellar—"

"Don't tout cots to a sybarite," Blixen said. He shook the
other's extended hand. "Wonderful seeing you again, John—"

"I suppose you'll be speaking to Karen."

"Yes—"

"Ask her to tell you about her father's—" MacVicar began, and
stopped.

"Her father's what?" Blixen inquired.

"Give her my love," MacVicar said. He pointed. "Oh-oh, here he comes—"

Blixen ran.

At the bottom of the path, he shaded his eyes against the downpour, but there was no bus to be seen. He squinted back at the white Victorian. The door was closed. It appeared to him that the peephole was open, although he could not see an eye at it.

Reflectively he forded the streaming street and splashed into the bus shelter, which was three-sided and open on the north to the bristling north wind.

On the hillock opposite him, the lights in MacVicar's windows were extinguished one by one.

Choppy, turreted, the old house sprawled against the sky like a Hitchcock exterior. Like the Transylvanian castle the young lovers always were directed to.

"But of course you must remain," insists the count in his liquid, red-lipped way. "It's true that I am not prepared for guests, but I could make up a nice grave in the basement."

Blixen smiled humorlessly and buried his chin in his upturned collar and jiggled his toes to keep them from freezing. The rain rattled on the shelter's roof; the wind sang in his ears. . . .

A nice grave, he thinks. What an apt proposal to make to a man lying dead in the Styx.

He sniffs. His nostrils have been offended by a strange odor. Newly turned earth. It reminds him of cemetery soil; it has a night crawler smell. The chunk-chunk beat of the digging has stopped. He raises his eyes to the figure crouched at the grave side with the shovel in its hands.

And he recognizes the face. He is as positive of that as the stroke victim is who recognizes that certain letters form certain words, without in the least understanding what the words mean. The shovel rolls in the murderer's grip; light stabs across Blixen's eyes. Revelation is on the tip of his mind. A ripping sound intrudes—

Startled, he woke. The ripping sound had become a transmission shifting up; the light—split into two lights—grew and glared. He thought *bus,* and blundered out of the shelter and raised his hand. But the lights boring toward him were lower and smaller than a bus's.

He dodged to his right, down the hill, fully expecting to be smacked flat. But the car had a curb to climb and that made all the difference. The hood caught him under the ribs. He floundered over a low iron fence onto a sodden lawn, landed on his knees and chin, thinking over and over: Check the license, the license, raise your head and note the *license*. But it was no use; he could not inveigle his muscles into a response. He toppled onto his side. The car had shouldered through the fence after him and had become stuck in the spongy grass. Now, while the engine whined and the car shook, doors up and down the block opened. The car rocked into reverse. The wheels sucked free. *License, dummy, license!* Blixen thought, but by the time he had forced his head to turn, the taillights were far down the hill.

He closed his eyes and spat dirt out of his mouth and considered what the flex of his neck signified. He was mobile; his back was not broken. He could twitch, spit, and breathe. Could he turn over? He focused his inner vision on the hypothesis, and saw himself turning, and turned. Suddenly the splatter—though not the sound—of the rain stopped; someone had opened an umbrella over his head. A circle of white faces gawked down. He concentrated on an Afro-haired young woman clutching the collar of a green bathrobe to her throat. "You'll catch cold," he said. A man in a cabbie's cap ducked close to him. "I radioed for an ambulance," he shouted. "Can you hear me?"

"I don't need an ambulance."

"Attaboy," bellowed the cabbie and patted his shoulder.

But it was true. Little by little he had begun to realize that the car had barely brushed him, that his wounds, dramatics notwithstanding, were shock-induced. Rage ached in his blood and bones. He had been violated by something bigger, stronger, dumber than he was, and his appetite for redress was consummate and biblical. "Tell me," he said and spat out another blade of grass.

"Huh?" said the cabbie.

"Tell me," Blixen tried again, "did anybody see what happened?"

"See it, I was right on his tail, you bet I seen it," said the cabbie.

"So did we, it was a gray Granada," stammered the Afro-haired girl. She elbowed a turbaned woman behind her. "Dodie, wasn't it?"

"Dark gray," Dodie confirmed. "There was mud all over the license plates but I think they were Oregon."

Blixen shifted his eyes to the cabbie. "Do you agree with that?"

"Yeah," the cabbie said. "Some half-assed sixteen-year-old out on the town, drunk as a skunk."

"You saw the driver?"

"I didn't have to, it's always some half-assed sixteen-year-old."

"Did *you* see him?" Blixen asked the Afro-haired girl.

"Well, sort of. He was kind of bent down, like a bike racer. I believe he had a cap or something on."

"A cap," Blixen repeated, and then: "Big nose?"

"You sound like you know him," Dodie said.

Blixen drew his feet out of a pool of water and said to the cab driver: "I wonder if I could go sit in your taxi for a minute, get out of this downpour."

"Be my guest," said the cabbie. "Can you move?"

"Sure, he just knocked the breath out of me."

"Take it easy—"

The fluid around Blixen's joints had congealed, but he was able to hoist himself upright without gasping.

"Everything work?" asked the cabbie.

"Everything that counts."

There was a good deal of distressed muttering from the gawkers, but they parted to let him shuffle past and seemed content to examine him through the windows when he sank into the back of the cab.

"All set?" asked the driver.

"Listen," Blixen said, "I'm not hurt. Why don't we forget the ambulance and just take off."

"Huh?" said the driver.

"Drop me at the Hilton."

"Hilton," repeated the driver. Rain fell in a steady stream off the brim of his cap. He clung to the top of the cab and inspected Blixen through the open rear door.

Blixen peered up. "Problems?"

"That's more or less what I'm trying to figure out," said the driver. "You take your average hit-and-run victim. He can't hardly wait to talk to the cops."

"I'll talk to them later," Blixen said. He prized his water-soaked wallet out of his inside coat pocket and peeled two fifties apart and held one out between the first two fingers of his right hand. "I just want to think some things over first."

"You figure," said the cab driver, "that he aimed at you deliberately, don't you?"

"I might. What's that got to do with you dropping me at the Hilton?"

"Well," said the driver, "I'm diabetic, I've got gallstones, and my blood pressure's one eighty over a hundred and ten. So the last thing in the world I need at this point in time is more trouble."

"Nobody'll give you trouble."

"How about your bike-racing, big-nosed friend?"

Blixen plucked the second fifty out of the wallet and tendered both bills. "Last offer."

The driver folded his lower lip over his upper, but made no move to accept the money.

"It was an accident," Blixen said. "But even if it wasn't, he's through for the night. You saw him light out of here."

Down the hill an approaching siren hooted and coughed.

"If he's through for the night," said the cabbie, "how come you want to split instead of going to emergency for tests or whatever?"

"I don't know," Blixen said. "Maybe I'm a Christian Scientist at heart."

The cab driver measured him, half-glanced toward the ambulance sounds, then reached out and pulled the two fifties free. He creased the bills lengthwise, tapped them against the top of the taxi, slipped them into his pocket. He walked around to the front of the cab and slid behind the wheel. "Tell me something," he said, "are you Mafia?" He ducked his head between his shoulders. "Scratch that," he said. He kicked the engine over, pulled out and away from the curb, and headed down Vista, past the oncoming ambulance. "Oh, me," he said.

But Blixen wasn't listening.

He had turned to keep the MacVicar Victorian in sight as long as possible. Not unexpectedly, the tumult had roused every house within shouting distance of the intersection. Except one. On the hillock, MacVicar's windows remained lightless and blind.

Slowly Blixen turned back, and crooked his fingers to keep them from stiffening, and thought, in his cab, about the stated lack of cabs on this busy, bleak night.

CHAPTER SEVEN

Dulcinea

I

By the time they had reached the Hilton's Sixth Street entrance, the downpour had modulated into a dogged mist. The driver, mindful perhaps of the Mafia as well as his hundred dollars, wished Blixen a courteous good evening and shot off around the corner onto Taylor like a half-assed sixteen-year-old.

Blixen shook his head and limped into the hotel.

The lobby was moist and crowded, almost impenetrable; nevertheless, he spotted her virtually at once and he stopped with the strangled snap of a dog on a short chain.

Her back was to him. She was talking to the desk clerk. She still had not learned to decorate herself; she wore a maroon warm-up jacket and pants and a pair of blue and yellow Nike jogging shoes. Her hair, short and dripping, looked as though it had been cut by a dull eggbeater. He had forgotten how tall she was. He collected his wits and started toward her, but before he had taken his second step, he had become engulfed in Japanese tourists and after he had extricated himself, he noticed that she had left the desk and was headed toward the Broadway exit. He hobbled forward. "Karen? Karen!"

She slowed doubtfully.

He dodged past a pennant-waving guide and surfaced before her. His next line was automatic. He couldn't help himself; it may have been the jogging shoes. "Not that way, dum-dum," he said.

Eyes wide, she began to laugh. She seemed poised to embrace him; her arms rose. But all the years had inhibited her. So he completed the bear hug himself, nuzzled her cold cheek, and she laughed again in delight. "What are you doing here?" Blixen exclaimed. "I called and called—"

"I work, I was at work!"

"I talked to Lucille—"

"I know! She invited me to the big reunion! She told me you were at the Hilton so I thought I'd run up first. . . . I live just down the block—Lincoln Tower—"

"You jog in the rain?"

"Rain, snow, every night. I'm as faithful as the postal service. Faithfuller. Your jaw's bleeding. And your coat's torn!"

"It's nothing. Zigged when I should have zagged. Please don't worry about it—"

"Do you mean to say," Karen exclaimed, "that you had the—the—the crazy courtesy to fly clear up to Portland for—whatever reason—and somebody mugged you?"

Choler made her glow; raindrops sparkled in her hair. Blixen realized now that he'd been premature in assuming that she'd arrived undecorated. The rain had played havoc with it, but he could see that she'd brushed on a little makeup: some lipstick, eyeshadow. For him? The fancy squeezed his heart. "How absolutely lovely you look," he said.

"Oh," she said, startled. "Well . . ." She managed a brief, cool smile, but before she could field the compliment, emotion betrayed her, and she burst into tears.

Startled in his turn, Blixen dug a clean, extra handkerchief out of his back pocket, pressed it upon her. "My dear girl—here—"

"Oh, isn't this squalid," Karen said into the handkerchief. "Oh, I hate people who do this! I'm embarrassing you."

"You're not."

"Throw your coat over my head and ignore me. I'll stop in a minute."

"Nonsense. Blow."

But she wouldn't. She just mopped her eyes and smudged the mascara and knocked one of her false eyelashes loose, which lent her the mussed aspect of a child gone amok at her mother's dressing table. She sucked in her breath and folded the handkerchief. "All right, Killer," she said, "now pull your socks up and act human. I mean it."

"Killer?"

She flashed him a strange look. "Don't jump, it's a nickname, not a tip-off." She picked the dangling eyelash free and stood staring at it.

"You know what we both need?" Blixen said. "A drink. A whole series of drinks. I'll see if I've had any calls, and then we'll go find a bar. I'll be right back."

He threaded his way through the lobby crowd to the front desk, aglow in spite of his bruised chest, and identified himself to the clerk. There were four message slips awaiting him, each of which bore the same telephone number and the same scribble: "Please call Mr. B. Lewis in Honolulu." He folded the messages, then returned to Karen's side.

She had found an empty chair, and dropped into it, and was peeling her other eyelash off when he walked up. She showed him the eyelash glumly. "Look at this," she said. "Sham, all sham. I can't imagine why I try these puerile tricks. Are you sure you feel all right? That's a terrible limp."

"Courting sympathy," Blixen said.

"Maybe we could postpone the drink until tomorrow."

"The drink, yes. The catching up, no."

She searched his face.

"The reminiscences," Blixen said. "The questions. The clarifications."

Karen inclined her head. "Of course. You're entitled."

Blixen said: "Why don't we go up to my room? I have a call to make. Then we can talk."

She continued to scrutinize him.

"Unless you have another appointment," Blixen said.

"Looking like this? Are you mad?"

She rubbed the heel of her hand over one grimy eye and rose and took his arm. "Some pair," she said. "The cripple and the Gorgon. Okay, carry on. . . ."

II

As it happened, he'd packed an extra jacket and a second pair of gray trousers, so he left Karen in the suite's sitting room while he washed the blood off his jaw and knees in the lavatory and donned his fresh clothes. An unexpected knob had risen over his temple.

He held a cold cloth against it, then tossed the cloth into the washbasin and returned to his guest.

She was standing by the window, watching the mist gather. She caught a glimpse of his reflection in the pane. "Pretty ritzy place you picked to bunk down in," she said.

"It's the studio's doing. I ask for a simple little cubicle somewhere, and this is what they reserve. The bar's stocked. Would you like that drink now?"

"I don't think so. The view alone's enough to make a person drunk. Mine's the other way. My view. West. Not nearly as attractive. I have a confession to make."

"About your view?"

"No, about me. You'd never guess it, because I project this sort of quintessential sophistication, but right now I'm a nervous wreck inside."

It drew a grin from him, until he realized that she was quite serious. "You are? Why?"

"I'm not sure." She fell silent. "Well, for one thing," she resumed, "I have a very heavy attitude toward dependence. I cannot abide being dependent. I never could."

"I remember."

"It used to drive my dad up the wall. I wouldn't take his hand when we crossed the street. He'd want to help me with my homework, and I'd close the book until he went away." She filled her lungs. "So what was the first thing I thought of doing when Detective Hitler braced me? Calling you for help. I've felt unnerved about that ever since."

"I've felt flattered about it ever since."

"And then to think that you'd come up here—all this way! I mean, you didn't even ask if I was guilty or not—"

"Are you guilty?"

"Well, no."

"There you are."

"And you believe me?"

"Of course."

"See, that just knocks me out."

"Why?"

"Because nobody *else* believes me. Sergeant Power certainly doesn't believe me."

"Sergeant Power has his own problems."

"He also doesn't believe you," Karen said. "He thinks we pre-arranged my alibi."

"But we didn't, so it doesn't matter what he thinks, does it."

"No," Karen said. Somewhere someone had turned on the tele-vision; they could hear a querulous rumbling, the faint, silly shriek of canned laughter. Rain peppered the window. Karen said reflec-tively: "Nils—"

"Yes."

"This seems to be my night for confessions."

"Does it?"

"I have another one to make."

Behind Blixen, the bar telephone trilled.

"Whew," Karen said. "There, I knew God wanted me to keep my mouth shut. Now we'll never know what an ass I might have made of myself."

She started away, but Blixen caught her arm. "What's your con-fession?"

"No, you answer your call," Karen said, and disappeared down the hall toward the bathroom.

Blixen contemplated his scuffed shoes through three more shrill yips, and then wheeled and yanked the phone off its cradle and snapped: "Yes! Yes! Hello!" into it.

Barney Lewis said: "Hello, who's this?"

"Why, this is the Pope," Blixen said. "Isn't that who you were calling?"

"Nils, this is Barn."

"No goddamn kidding."

"I'll bet I caught you in the shower or something," Barney said.

Blixen sighed. Even the slightest receiver pressure hurt his right ear.

"Well, hey, this can wait," Barney continued. "You go towel off and we'll—"

"Barn," Blixen cut in, "what you caught me on was a very short string. I apologize for barking at you."

"That's exactly why I haven't tried to go back to my own home town in over thirty years," Barney said. "Those short strings. Would you care to discuss it?"

"No. Tell me what's happening in Honolulu."

"All right. Where to start?"

"Start with Roland," Blixen began, but before he'd finished the sentence, a voice in the background broke in to cry: "Start! I'll tell you where to start! You tell that—"

"Here, you talk to him," Barney said over his shoulder.

"I don't want to talk to him! Screw the son of a bitch!"

"There could only be one voice in the world as dulcet as that," Blixen said. "My star. The Emmy's Home Companion. Put him on, Barn."

"Murphy, take the phone, he wants to say hello," Barney said. "Will you take the *phone! Take* it!"

Pregnant pause.

"*Maître!*" cried Murphy Smith.

"Murf!" Blixen cried back.

"Well, what's the good word, Nils! You wouldn't believe how hot the Islands are. I'll bet the Northwest's lovely this time of year."

"Couldn't be lovelier," Blixen agreed. "What did the doctor say?"

Again the pregnant pause bellied up. Even larger this time. Twins, perhaps.

"Hello?" Blixen said.

"You hate me, don't you?" Murf said.

"Did you see the doctor?"

"Answer my question."

"No, I don't hate you, Murphy. I admire you. You're durable, you wear well on the screen, you carry responsibilities and a work load that would kill the average man. What I hate are the babyish stratagems you use to try to get your own way."

"If you saw a man tottering on a ledge," Murf burst out, "staggering and fainting and yelling for help, would you try to save him, or would you stand there and criticize his stratagems?"

"But you aren't on a ledge, you're in the kiddies' sandbox."

"I am *falling!*" Murf bellowed.

"Murphy—"

"I am about to hit bottom, oh yes, yes, and you don't care! What's the matter with you? Do you want to lose this pukey series? Help me, Nils! Just because I look like Peter Falk doesn't mean I can't hurt inside! I hurt!"

Blixen said patiently: "Murf, you hurt because a talented director has asked you to dig beneath the obvious, to search for—"

"Horseshit!" Murf bawled, and uttered a wild laugh. "Talented? Why, that overripe old fart couldn't direct a rat to the cheese! He goes to sleep on the set and everybody flounders because they're afraid to wake him up and ask him what to do next!"

"Who else flounders? Isabel?"

"Señorita Chavez, *cher maître,* is too fat to flounder. Señorita Chavez just stands there and mumbles her lines in her Chicana singsong and sweats."

"Donald Gould?"

"Oh, forget Donald! The important—"

"In other words," Blixen said, "the only actor Rolly can't break through to is you."

"Listen to me! Listen!" Murf shouted. "This series lives or dies on *my* performance! Mine! Nobody else's! And I cannot WORK with that putteed bastard! Every time he yells at me I curl up inside like an amelinee—amela—what is it? In the aquariums—the stalks—"

"Anemone."

"I can't say that. Will you replace him?"

"Phipps? No."

"Nils—oh, Jesus. All right, I'm going home."

"You do and you're out," Blixen said.

Silence throbbed over the line.

In the ornate mirror behind the bar, Blixen saw Karen emerge from the hallway. Her face was washed and wan, her hair more or less combed. She had unzipped the maroon warm-up jacket; beneath it she wore a T-shirt that said STASSEN FOR PRESIDENT across the chest. She perched on a bar stool at the end of the counter and picked at some salted peanuts in a silver bowl. Blixen smiled at her, but her face remained grave.

"Do you know what I think?" Murphy asked.

"You think I'm bluffing," Blixen said.

"I think you're bluffing," Murf said, "and I'll tell you why. If I'm terminated, the series is terminated. And no producer over the age of twelve would be crazy enough to throw the baby out with the bathwater. Would he?"

"We'll find out the minute you leave."

Incredulously Murphy cried: "Do you mean to say that you'd wreck a successful series just to break an actor's spirit?"

"No," Blixen said. "But I'd end a successful series before I'd allow an actor or anyone else to dictate the terms for its survival."

"But I'm RIGHT!"

"Not in my opinion."

"How can you have an opinion? You're not here, you don't see what that maniac's up to, you sit on your pompous butt and close your eyes to the truth and then you deliver your judgment like the oracle from Philadelphia! Do you call that fair?"

Karen split a peanut and ate the part at the tip that resembled a miniature bearded head and dropped the rest into a clean ashtray. She propped her chin in her hand and nipped the bearded head out of a fresh peanut and discarded the remainder of that one, too. She caught Blixen gazing at her, and offered him the peanut dish. He shook his head.

"Nils?" Murf said.

"Go ahead, I'm listening," Blixen said.

"Oh, you are not, what's the use," Murphy groaned. All of a sudden he sounded as whipped and bitter as a child sent to bed without TV. "You had your mind made up before you ever hired that freak. You're on Phipps's side and you always were."

Still with his eyes on Karen, Blixen said: "True. But that isn't the point, Murphy. The point—and I thank you for reminding me of it—is that my preconceptions have no God-given right to ride roughshod over your preconceptions. We both believe we have a stranglehold on the truth. But my position is defendable, and yours isn't, and I'm not afraid to prove it."

Karen glanced up.

"And how do you expect to do that," Murf argued, "sitting three thousand miles away in some—"

"I don't. We need a face-to-face discussion. I'll set one up."

Murf said: "Oh."

"Let me speak to Barn."

"Barn?" Murphy repeated vaguely. And then he must have held the phone out without another word because Barney Lewis came back on at once.

"Yes, Nils."

"I'm flying over."

(In the mirror Blixen watched Karen slide off the bar stool and walk to the window and stand, diminished and still, against the rainy black sky.)

"You," Barney said, "have just made my day. Praise the Lord. Flying over when?"

"I'll let you know as soon as I book the flight. Sometime Sunday."

"I'll reserve you a room."

"I won't need a room. I'll only be there for a couple of hours. I still have a good deal to do here."

(In the mirror, Karen folded her arms and clamped her fingers over her biceps.)

"Set up a meeting at the hotel," Blixen went on. "You, Rolly, Murf, Isabel—"

"Nils, I'm sorry you have to make the trip, but I don't think there's any other way to resolve this mess."

"Neither do I. See you Sunday."

Blixen lowered the receiver and dialed the hotel operator. To the figure at the window, he said: "Forgive me. One more quick call."

"Disaster in fantasy-land?" Karen murmured.

"A little misunderstanding."

The hotel operator said: "Operator—"

"Hello," Blixen said. "I'd like to talk to somebody at police headquarters—Central Precinct—Homicide Division. I'll speak to whoever's there." He switched the phone to his other ear and stroked the knob on his temple. Karen hadn't stirred.

The phone clicked. "Homicide. Vandenburgh."

"Sergeant Power, please."

"Sergeant Power's not in the office at the moment. Can I help you?"

"I hope so. My name's Blixen—and—I was in the sergeant's car earlier, and I think I may have left my wallet there. Brown leather. Smooth—"

"Nobody's called in about any wallet, Mr. Glicksman, but I'll write Sergeant Power a note and no doubt he'll contact you. Better give me your number."

"Would he have gone home after dropping me off?"

"No, sir, he'd have checked in here."

"I hate to keep on and on about this," Blixen said, "but every scrap of identification I own is in that wallet. Is it possible that he could have changed cars in the course of the evening? In other words, do you people ever bring one car in for some reason—oh, say you bang up a fender—and then sign another one out? I'd hate to think of my wallet sitting there overnight in the police garage. I remember the car. I didn't notice the color, but it was a four-door Granada—"

"That would be the gray job," Vandenburgh said.

Blixen said: "The gray job, right."

"Why don't you give me your number, Mr. Glicksman—"

"Or wait, here's a thought," Blixen interrupted. "Suppose I come over to the garage and look for the wallet myself? If Connie hasn't returned the car yet, I'll wait for him. Can I do that?"

"No," said Vandenburgh. "Where did you say you were calling from, sir?"

"Oh, hold the fort," Blixen exclaimed, "hold everything, I found it!"

Laconically Vandenburgh said: "I'll be darned."

"It was in my briefcase. Sorry I bothered you—"

"Sir, any time," Vandenburgh said and expelled air hard through his nose and hung up.

Blixen bumped the dead phone twice against the point of his jaw, cradled it and ate some of Karen's beheaded peanuts. When he lifted his eyes to the mirror he saw that she had turned and was watching him thoughtfully. He swung around on his bar stool. "Finished," he said. "No more calls. Let's talk about you."

"Boy, for a member of the establishment you really carry on some weird conversations," Karen said.

"You ought to hear me when I'm dealing with the networks." There was a sealed fifth of J&B at the end of the counter. Blixen cracked it, lifted it, but she shook her head no and he poured a single shot, neat, for himself. He took a sip, and positioned the glass in the exact center of a white cocktail napkin. "Karen," he said, "what do you know about Conrad Power?"

"Virtually nothing, I'm thankful to say. Why?"

"Do you remember him at Grant?"

"I didn't realize he'd gone to Grant—"

"You never turned him down at a dance? Laughed at his big nose? Anything like that?"

"No." She tilted her head. "Are you serious?"

Blixen tapped a fingernail against the rim of his glass, finally swept it up, drained it. "Halfway," he said. "The other half could be paranoia."

"Why on earth should Power make you paranoid? I'm the one he's accused of murder."

"Yes, but I'm the one he may have tried to kill tonight." Karen's fingers continued to bite into her biceps. Her eyes remained intent on his. The scotch glowed in Blixen's stomach. "I believe I must have taken you somewhat aback," he said.

"*Kill* you?"

"I was at a bus stop in the West Hills. A gray Granada tried to run me down. Power knew I was in the neighborhood. He drove me there. In a gray Granada."

"Well—but accidents sometimes—"

"The car followed me over the curb and through a fence. It was no accident."

"And you're sure Sergeant Power was driving it?"

"No, I'm not," Blixen said. "Which is where the paranoia comes in. I may be on the wrong track altogether."

"But if it was Power's car, it would be banged up. Is that what you were checking on?"

"Yes."

Karen dropped her arms. "I see." She wiped her palms across her hips and stared at the carpet. "I *say* I see, but I don't. Could I have that drink after all?"

"Of course. Scotch?"

"Please."

Blixen poured another finger of J&B for each of them, carried Karen's glass to her, and tipped his own. "Confusion to the enemy," he said.

Saluting, Karen tossed off the drink. It proved to be hotter than she'd expected and she huffed a little in order to cool her singed throat. When she'd caught her breath she croaked: "Question time."

"Shoot."

"First of all, no matter how I slice it, Nils, I cannot for the life of me understand why you think Conrad Power would want to kill you. I mean, even paranoia has to have some base—"

"Do you understand why he'd want to hound you for a murder you didn't commit?"

"In a way I do. He's a cop, and he's under pressure. Either he jails somebody for Sophocles' murder, or his own career goes down the drain."

"But why jail you in particular?"

"Because I'm the likeliest suspect. After all, I did threaten Sophocles."

"Half of Portland must have threatened him. Sophocles Kanaris begged to be threatened. He was a deadbeat, a bigot, a rapist, a pusher—" Blixen hesitated. "Did you know that, by the way?"

Karen, who had bent aside to search for a place to set down her empty glass, glanced back. "Know he was a drug dealer? Yes, I knew that. Mick was an addict. He told me Sophocles was his source. He said Sophocles' supply was the best on the market. He offered to sell me some."

"And did you buy?"

"No."

"All right," Blixen said, "now if—"

Karen said: "There you go believing me again."

"Shouldn't I?"

"Of course you *should*. The point—"

She hesitated.

"Maybe the point," Blixen said, "is that you can't believe me when I say it."

Her eyes searched his.

Blixen said: "Karen—you know—that little girl who wouldn't take her father's hand crossing the street—I find that little girl terribly touching. I think it must be a very hard thing for a child never to dare to be dependent. Never to trust an extended hand. Never to expect the net to be there when she falls. I wonder how it happened?"

"I don't want to talk about this," Karen said. "Please stop it." She began a tour of the room, pausing here and there to examine a particularly repellent objet d'art. Her hair had fallen forward over her eyes. She spread it in order to inspect a Dresden shepherdess who had somehow gotten her crook stuck up a lamb's nose. "All right," she said distantly, "so any number of people might have hated Sophocles enough to want to kill him. But that's just theory. I wish you'd name me some names."

"How about John MacVicar? I talked to John tonight. He still blames Sophocles for Mick's addiction."

Slowly, dissatisfied, Karen said: "Yes—but still—"

"Or can't you accept John as the type who might want to square accounts?"

Sighing, Karen said: "Oh, I suppose I can. At least he seems capable of it now. But was he then? He's changed, Nils. Sure, now he's all blood and thunder and high passion. He's been through analysis. But don't you remember how bland he was as a kid? Compared to Mick? Could you imagine *that* John stabbing somebody to death?"

"It does require a certain effort," Blixen agreed. "Although having an addict in the family might make anyone emotional. . . . Incidentally, were there any others in our neighborhood?"

"Addicts? I don't think so. Not among the girls I was close to anyhow. Maybe some pot smokers."

"Did Lucille smoke marijuana?"

"Never," Karen said. "I thought it might be fun, but she'd read somewhere that it would rot our noses off and turn our brains mushy. I think she mixed it up with VD."

"How about Coco?"

"Coco," Karen asserted, "would have tried anything including sex with a salamander if she thought it might feel good."

"Then that gives us three more suspects."

"How?"

"Suppose Sophocles had introduced Coco to heroin. It's not unheard of for an addict to attack her supplier."

"That's one. You said three."

"Or for an addict's parents to attack her supplier."

"Gilbert? *Agnes?*"

"Mrs. DeForrest had had a very emotional day."

"But it was her husband she was emotional about! If she'd set out to kill anybody it would have been him!"

"Maybe she killed them both."

"Right," Karen said. "Stuck a knife into Sophocles and then

rushed off to Chicago and infected old Gilbert with cancer cells."
She regarded Blixen gloomily. "Who else do you have on this extraordinary list of yours?"

"Everyone who was at the party. And some who weren't."

"Mick?"

"Yes, definitely."

"Lucille? Clem?"

"Yes."

"Which one?"

"Both."

"Nils, come on! You'll be suspecting Santa Claus next. Clem and Lucille Gompers are the two most moral people I know—"

"Who'd flip harder over immorality than the ultra moral? Lucille still remembers a pinch Sophocles laid on her at the Hamburger Hut. Maybe it was the straw that broke the camel's back. Maybe she realized what Sophocles was doing to Mick MacVicar. And maybe she decided that the world would be better off without a man like that."

"If she had she would have prayed extra hard for God to change his wicked ways. Besides, Clem swears she was smooching with him at the beach when Sophocles was killed. How do you get around that?"

"Can't sell you on Lucille then," Blixen said. "Well, I'm not surprised. That's why I saved the best for the last."

"Who's left?" She ticked off the names. "You, me, John, Mick, Coco, the DeForrests, Lucille and Clem. . . . Isn't that the lot?"

"Not quite. You're forgetting everybody's pal. The cop with the missing gray Granada—"

"Power?" She threw up her hands. "Well, I give up on you! *Power?* Nils, the man didn't even know Sophocles!"

"Sophocles," Blixen pointed out, "peddled his wares from Irvington to Parkrose. He was the root source of pornography in the area. He fenced stolen property, and he dealt in drugs. He scalped tickets. He probably pimped. There is no way that any young male at Grant High could have been unaware of him. Conrad Power went to Grant."

"And that's your case?"

"Not all of it," Blixen said. "You doubted a connection and

I've given you a possible one." He indicated the knob on his temple. "No, *this* is my ace-in-the-hole. The attempt on my life."

"Nils—look—I understand how you feel, but, honestly, it's so illogical! If you could just explain to me why Power—or anybody else—would want to run you down. . . . I mean, if you'd done something to him, or—"

"But it isn't what I did," said Blixen, "it's what I saw."

He had caught her on the upbeat. Admonishing finger raised, she had been prepared to punch home any number of trenchant objections. Now he could nearly hear her mind change gears. Slowly she said: "I don't understand. What could you see that—"

"The murder," Blixen said.

She lowered her finger.

"Well, let's be accurate," Blixen said. "What I saw was Sophocles in the open grave. I caught the murderer burying him."

She remained stock-still, as motionless as a raccoon observing a wolf drink on the opposite bank of a pond.

"Now it's question time for sure, isn't it?" Blixen said.

The wolf lapped; the raccoon watched.

"For instance," Blixen continued, "if I witnessed the killing—or its aftermath—or any part of it—why on earth would I keep so quiet about it for so long?"

Karen whispered: "Oh, I can think of a better question than that."

"Like—?"

"Who was filling in the grave?"

"I don't know."

"You have a very selective memory."

"I have a very capricious memory," Blixen said. "It goes its own way. Or it did that night. Too much beer—too much blood. It didn't come back to me until about an hour and a half ago."

"And—what finally brought it back?"

"Bad dreams and a little probing."

Karen stuck her hands into the pockets of her jogging pants and sat on the edge of a stiff chair and considered her extended legs. "Maybe," she said at last, "you never did see the grave digger. Is that possible?"

"I saw him," Blixen replied. "I can see him yet. Him and his shovel. It's misty, but the face is there."

"You keep saying 'him.' But it could have been anybody."

"Yes."

"Including me."

"Yes."

Her hands had begun to work in her pockets, to bunch up, form fists. She became aware of it, removed the hands, crossed her knees and linked her fingers around the upper one. "Nils," she said, "I wonder—are we ever going to discuss the main problem? Or are we just going to let it sit there and nag at us?"

"And what do you consider the main problem to be?"

She made herself look at him. Her eyes, behind the half-closed lids, were enigmatic. She seemed to be waiting for him to give her a nudge, to wind her up, to set her off again. But he wouldn't do that. And when she realized once and for all that he wouldn't, she said in a curious tone: "You need to have me blurt it straight out, don't you, all by myself."

"Yes."

She let a few more seconds pass, and then she sighed and said: "Okay. The *main* problem—from my point of view—is—that I lied through my teeth this morning." She shot a glance at him, but his face remained implacably placid. "I lied to Floyd Duffield," she went on. "I lied to Power. I lied to you when we phoned. Because of course I'd panicked. I didn't have an alibi. We hadn't spent the whole night together." Her pose on the chair's edge was casual and relaxed, but her plaited fingers were bloodless. "Although I don't believe you remembered that at the time."

"I didn't."

"I could tell. You sounded so hearty and positive that I was sure you were backing me up out of blind faith. So tonight I thought I'd better confess the truth to you no matter what. And I would have, if the phone hadn't rung. You were still in the dark and I couldn't stand that."

"The fact is that I still am in the dark."

For a second the rise and fall of her breast stopped altogether.

Blixen nodded. "It's true. I can remember the grave side and some of what happened there, and I can recall a good deal of the party. But there are gaps in between. I don't remember leaving your house, for instance."

"Leaving the bedroom?"

"Were we in your bedroom?"

She gaped at him. "Were we in—!" She sank back in the chair. "Well, for Pete's sake," she said flatly. "Well, there goes the Playmate image. Where are you, Hugh Hefner, when I need you?"

In the charred fireplace, the flames leap and ebb. The bare floor is unkind to his naked knees. His pants and shirt hang over a basket half full of chopped wood. His lips touch her silken belly.

"Take your socks off," she whispers. "No gentleman wears his socks at a time like this."

"How do you know?"

"I read a lot."

The socks join the pants and the shirt.

She seems hypnotized. "Look at the size of you."

He feels strong as a giant. He places one arm under her shoulders, the other beneath her knees. He remembers to lift with his legs.

"What's all this?" she demands.

"The floor's too hard. Where's your bedroom?"

She leans her cheek on his shoulder. "Straight back, first door on the left—"

"On the left!" Blixen exclaimed. "Your bed was against the far wall, under an open window—!"

"Forget it, you're too late, you had your chance," Karen grumbled.

"The bedspread was yellow and you had pictures of Francina Blankers-Koen on your dresser! Any other girl would have collected movie stars' photos, but you went for Francina Blankers-Koen."

"Because she was a great champion—nineteen forty-eight Olympics. Hundred-meter run—two hundred meters—eighty-meter hurdles—"

Dotted swiss curtains flutter in the night wind, caress Francina Blankers-Koen's pugnacious Dutch face. The dew-heavy scent of freshly cut grass breaks Blixen's heart; Mr. Chaplin, that crazy iconoclast, has mown his lawn on a Friday instead of waiting until the weekend like your normal Portlander. Well, the fact is that Blixen, in his fulfilled and contented state, would have forgiven Chaplin anything, defended the man to the death. He feels a sacred link to all the Chaplins now; he has possessed the Chaplin heiress; he is part of the tribe. Satiated, he flops onto his left side, throws his right leg across his girl's warm bed. . . . His toes explore, but find only sheet. He sits bolt upright. He is alone. . . .

He realized suddenly that she'd been speaking to him. "I'm sorry—what?"

"It's coming back to you, isn't it."

Bereft, hollering her name, hopping on one foot as he struggles into his pants, he seeks her in the butter-colored kitchen, in the living room, even in the basement—

"Nils, what are you remembering?"

"That empty house. I woke up alone. I looked for you everywhere."

"Not everywhere."

"Everywhere I could think of."

"I was in the loft," Karen explained in a low voice. "It was my secret place. When the world got too big for me, I'd climb up there and look at the moon—and—I don't know—"

"Wait for the spinning to stop."

"Yes." She examined him out of the corner of her eyes. "And there'd been spinning enough to make a dervish dizzy that night. It was the first time I'd been with a man. And he'd fallen asleep on me—"

One of her shoelaces had come undone—or she thought it had— or she pretended it had. She bent forward to attend to it, and her hair fell across her eyes again, and Blixen placed his cupped palm over the back of her head, the round, perfect, remembered skull shape. She turned to him. He drew her nearer. Eyes closed, she accepted the tug of his hand, the weight of his mouth on hers. She whispered: "Nils," against his lips, and held his own head close in the crook of her left arm.

"You have the most beautiful skull," Blixen murmured, "that God ever made."

Half an inch from his left eye, her right eye opened. "Skull?"

"Secretly, I have had the hots for your skull for years," Blixen said.

"What do you aim to do to it?"

"Just hold it like this."

"Holy smoke," Karen said. "Here I am, friendless and alone,

twenty-two stories in the air, at the mercy of a skull freak. Mama."

"No use calling for help, my lovely," Blixen said. "No one can hear you now."

III

Later, lying on his slack arm in the enormous bed, cheek resting against his, she told him: "I could hear *you*, though."

After a moment, he shifted his head to gaze at her.

"I could hear *you*," she repeated. "Calling my name that night."

"Oh."

"But by the time I climbed down from the loft, you were gone."

Shapes form and falter in his mind, side-slip, dissolve. He plods stubbornly toward the DeForrest house—

"Why did you leave like that, Nils?"

Why had he? His mouth had been dry as dust; he'd felt abandoned, thirsty, deprived. "I believe I must have been after the beer," he said.

Up the DeForrest bank he stalks. There is not a light on anywhere in the house. Nevertheless someone must be about. He can hear slurred sounds on the driveway—a thick chunk-chunking. He slips past a shrub, around a corner. Sophocles lies in his grave; the figure above lifts its shovel—

"Did you ever find it?" Karen asked.

"Find what?"

"The beer you went after."

"No, I didn't find it."

"Nils, you're shivering. Wait—you've kicked the blanket off—"

"I can't see his face!"

"All right, just—"

"He stands there like an ape, and he shakes his shovel—and I can't see him!"

"Yes, darling, but you will. It's safe there in your mind." Her voice was as hypnotic as her fingertips at his groin. "Give it a while—"

The frustration seeped away. He stretched and relaxed his legs, rotated his neck muscles, allowed her knowledgeable fingers to soothe him. He kissed her eyelids and found them wet. He lifted himself on his elbows. "Are you crying?"

"Where did you go after that?"

"Tell me why you're crying."

"Because we were all so young. And because it could have been such a beautiful night, and it went so totally to pieces."

"I never did come back to you, did I."

"No."

"Were you worried?" Blixen asked. "Mad?"

"Scared and mad. I fell asleep in front of the fire, and when I woke up and you still weren't there, I phoned your house. It was about four in the morning. No one answered."

"My parents had gone to Seattle."

"But where had *you* gone?"

Where? No use. "I don't know. . . ."

Still, there is something fussing at him, gathering, a sneeze of a thought that refuses to mature. . . . Someone has begun to shout. His ears cringe. His mother weeps. He is lying in his own crusty vomit, watching a wave of water arch languidly toward him out of a galvanized pail. Somehow it has the repetitive persistence of a film loop. It is as though he has spent half his days stretched flat on his back being bellowed at and attacked. He cannot, in the grip of his graduation hangover, remember where or why or with whom he had fought before; anyway his concern now is with drowning rather than amnesia. The arching water is nearly upon him. At the last second, he struggles aside. He pays a fearful price in nausea, but most of the pail's contents miss him, although he does get the back splash and the point: His father wants him awake and on his feet. His mother wants everybody to shut up for the neighbors' sake, but his father wants an explanation. Nils staggers erect. He is in his own bathroom. It is a bright Saturday and his parents have just returned from Seattle. Outrage thickens the air. For years, a showdown between Nils and his father had been foretold by the rest of the family. They are too individualistic, Nils and Thor Blixen. Compromise has rubbed them both raw, and now there is no skin left to abrade. To the forty-five-year-old Thor, this seventeen-year-old child is a frail and lazy reed, a drone, a disappointment, a smart-ass. Thor had not wanted to leave the boy unsupervised on graduation night. He had groused about it to his wife all the way to Seattle, and had warned her all the way back to expect to find their home gutted when they returned. Bottles, he predicted, would litter the lawn. Girls' pants would festoon the chandeliers and unspeakable objects would clog the toilet. It has not been quite as bad as that (there were no girls' pants in evidence, and the toilet still worked) but the glass door of the locked liquor cabinet had been smashed in and a bottle each of gin, Bourbon, and vodka had either been broken or consumed, presumably by Nils alone. Hanging onto the towel rack, Nils tries to reassemble the last few shattered hours, and fails altogether. He recalls attending the graduation party, but how, or why, or when he had left it is lost in a fog of alcohol fumes. Now and then Karen's face swoops reproachfully past. He supposes that he has insulted her. In a day or two he will pluck up his courage and ask her how he has misbehaved himself, and will undergo whatever penance is appropriate. Meanwhile, here is his mother tottering around in tears and his father sawing the air like a German bandleader and screaming Scandinavian curses. It is a critical moment. If ever the fossilized ties between father and son are to snap, it will be now. To his horror, it is Nils who makes them snap. At the top of his lungs he suddenly roars out an expletive of such hair-raising obscenity that he cannot credit his own ears. For an astounded second, no one moves; even his wet-faced mother stops gulping. Then Nils becomes preternaturally aware of two things: the broken red veins in his father's eyes—and the wiry hairs on the knuckles of the fist aimed at him. This time he cannot dodge away. He is hit on the left side of the mouth, driven backward into the tub on his behind. His lip is split; a tooth is loosened. He doesn't see stars; he sees those knuckle hairs. He sprawls in the tub and sucks his bloody lip and thinks with crystalline clarity: I'm going to kill that man. But three facts prevent it. First, his father already has left the bathroom. Second, his mother keeps him pinned impotently in the bathtub. Third, he's scared that the old man may come back and hit him again, even harder. He snarls and threatens, but behind it all is a relief so colossal as to render him light-headed. Great decisions have been made; gates have clanged shut. By one-thirty that afternoon, he is on the Greyhound bus to L.A. He never thinks twice about it, he never looks back, he never sees his father alive again. In sunny southern California, he catches cold after cold, and by the time he's found a job and his balance, half the summer has passed and he has not yet contacted anyone in Portland, even Karen. One day on the beach at Santa Monica, he writes her a note of explanation and apology, largely incoherent, but even though he haunts the General Delivery window in Culver City, where he has found a room, he never hears from her. Never hears from her—never forgets her . . .

IV

His watch lay on the bedside table at the base of the extension phone; the glowing green hands pointed to ten minutes past three. The rain had stopped. The night breathed peacefully. Silence, Blixen had learned from his rerecording crew, was never quite silent. To add silence to a scene, one opened a microphone in an empty room, and made a tape of the hush there, and added that to the track. Even the brain of a deaf man is stuffed with squeaks and clickings, surf-booms, remembered voices. *Not that way, dum-dum. . . .*

"Do you know where I made my mistake?" Blixen asked.

Karen had fallen asleep. Her ankle twitched against his. Blixen could feel her wondering where she was—and then realizing, and relaxing. "Mistake?" she muttered.

"On the day I left Portland—on that Saturday afternoon—I should have phoned you from the Greyhound station, and asked you to come with me. Would you have?"

"I probably wouldn't even have spoken to you."

"It's strange. I knew something wonderful and terrible had happened—but I couldn't remember what. I'd had a fight with my parents—"

"Yes, you wrote me." She sighed and found a new position; her breath warmed his chest. "I wish I'd been able to answer your letter—"

"Why couldn't you?" Blixen asked.

"I couldn't do much of anything that summer. I felt as if I'd fallen into a volcano." Her fingers lay listlessly on his hipbone. "One big blast after another. If I wasn't graduating or learning about sex, I was blaming myself—"

"For learning about sex?"

"That, and I suppose for you leaving. And of course for my dad. . . ."

Blixen frowned at the shadow play on the ceiling. "You felt guilty about your dad?"

"For what he did, sure."

It mystified him. "Well, what did he—"

"For his *death*, Nils. He died. You knew that."

It shocked him. "No. I didn't. When?"

"That June. Toward the end of June."

"Good God." Compassion flooded through him. "What a terrible summer for you. Was it his heart?"

"It was his neck," Karen said. "He got up one Sunday, and he climbed into my loft and he hanged himself. I found him. I helped my mother cut him down. But he was cold by then. We couldn't have saved him."

She might have been discussing a side of beef. Her head was beneath Blixen's jaw, but her voice seemed to come from galactic distances away. "He'd been too quiet the night before. I half expected he'd try something dumb. I never did trust him."

Chaplin. That damned showboat. That guider of schoolchildren and gentler of scared animals. That husband, father, Dracula. . . .

"I told you I had a very heavy attitude toward dependence," Karen added.

Over and over the little girl twists away from her father's hand, closes her homework, cuts through the rope. Never did trust him. Poor little girl.

He had said it aloud.

"Don't cry, we managed," Karen replied. "The business was in good shape. We turned it from a dog hospital into a pet shop. My featherheaded mother would argue religion with the parrots and I'd handle the accounts. I still have the store. Chaplin and Gogarty, on Fourth."

"Who's Gogarty?"

"Gogarty?" said Karen. "Gogarty is my cross and also my partner. Up until last July, he was also my roommate. We still see each other at work five days a week. We're very correct toward each other at work. I call him 'Dr. Gogarty,' and he calls me 'Killer.'"

"So that's where the nickname comes from."

"Yeah. We were in a motel in southern Oregon one summer, and a mosquito got in. I wouldn't let him swat it. I captured it in a glass jar and turned it loose outside. He's called me 'Killer' ever since."

"You sound very fond of Gogarty."

"I'm not in the least fond of him. He wanted too much from me."

"Like what? Trust?"

She closed her mouth so hard that her teeth snapped. After a while she reopened it to say: "Nils, please spare me your profundities. I'm not in the mood. Let's just change the subject."

"Tell me about your father then."

"I already have. He lived thirty-eight irresponsible years, and he killed himself."

"That's a very sad epitaph."

"Well, it's the sad truth."

Something had turned her prickly. Her body continued to huddle close to him, but spiritually she had begun to edge off. Why? he wondered. Because of his questions about Gogarty? Or because she already had revealed too much about her dangling dead father?

"Karen—"

Yawning, she complained: "Oh, Nils, I'm really worn out. It must be three o'clock. Let's talk about it in the morning." She kissed his nose and flopped onto her stomach. She buried her face in her pillow, and exhaled hugely.

"Karen," Blixen said, "why did your dad kill himself?"

Her voice was muffled and sleepy. "Sweetheart, I haven't the faintest idea."

"Did he and Sophocles know each other?"

Silence.

"On the night of the murder—when Sophocles came to your house—was it to see you? Or your dad?"

"Who told you," Karen murmured, "that Sophocles came to my house that night?"

"John MacVicar. He said he saw Sophocles come out of your side door."

She removed her face from the pillow, rested her cheek on the back of her hand, and inspected him.

Blixen said: "Karen—let me lay this thing out for you as flat as I can." He marshaled his thoughts. "As of now—and until I can remember who and what I saw on the DeForrest driveway—you're Power's pigeon. He's nearly ready to ask for an indictment. That means the case is provable, as far as he's concerned."

"Floyd Duffield told me," Karen said, "that any prosecutor who tried to build a case on the silly threats I made that evening would be laughed out of court. He said that if I'd wanted to kill Sophocles, I'd have done it then. When I was up to it emotionally—"

"I agree."

"Then I can't imagine—"

"Which means," Blixen overrode her, "that Power thinks he can convince the D.A. that you had another motive, a stronger one."

"He's *mental,* that man!"

"MacVicar backs him up," Blixen said.

"Nils, I swear to you—!"

"No, don't swear," Blixen said. "Don't cross your heart and hope to die. Don't play any more games. Just tell me the truth."

Shocked, she shut her mouth; her eyes flicked back and forth across his.

"Why did Sophocles come to your house graduation night?"

"I'm going home," Karen said. She threw her legs over the side of the bed and sat up. In the half-light, her slender bare back seemed ghostlike, insubstantial. Her hands lay palms up in her lap, loose and forgotten; she was crying.

Blixen touched his knuckles to the swell of her hip.

But she remained unresponsive, drawing neither closer nor away, lost in some limbo of her own making.

Blixen whispered: "My darling, we're at a very basic crossroads here. If all you need from me is faith and support and compassion, I'll give them to you gladly and I'll not bug you again. But if it's my help you want, I must have something in return."

The shake of her head was so minute he couldn't be sure he'd seen it.

"You don't want my help?" he asked.

"I do, but I can't pay those prices."

"All I'm asking for is candor and a little trust."

"That's everything."

After a moment Blixen said: "Maybe it is."

"I liked you better when you were baying after Sergeant Power."

"I still am."

"But if you're so convinced he's the killer, why do you—"

"But I'm not convinced of it. Suspicion isn't proof. Power may be as innocent as a newly washed kitten."

"He's not, he's malicious and inflexible and crazy." She rubbed the back of one hand across her eyes and sat looking at the other hand in her lap. "Nils," she resumed, "how old were you when you first tried to swim?"

"Five or six, I can't remember."

"I was nine. One Saturday my dad drove me out to the pool at Jantzen Beach, the deep one. He let me float around in my life preserver for a couple of minutes and then he took it away from me and he told me to let go of the side of the tank. He treaded water and asked me to dog-paddle over to him. But I couldn't. We went out there for six straight Saturdays. But I could never let go of the side of the tank."

"What did you think would happen to you?"

"I was sure I'd drown. I'm drowning now."

"But," Blixen said, "every swimmer alive feared he'd drown when he first let go. It's part of the cost."

"Then I won't pay it."

"Then you'll never learn to swim."

She examined her fingernails, and put her face in her hands and sank back onto the bed beside him, still with her face covered. Through her cupped hands, she said: "You're a TV producer, Nils. You deal in scenarios. Tell me what you think of this one: I do as you ask. I reveal all my little secrets. And you spill them to Power. And it turns out that Power has been lying all along, that he never did have a case—until you and I presented him with one.

And I end up in the state penitentiary for a crime I didn't commit."

Presently Blixen said: "And that's the scenario you see, is it?"

"In my nightmares, yes."

"You must be sitting on some pretty wild secrets."

"Wild." She tried the word on her tongue. "Well, no, I wouldn't say wild so much as dingy. The kinds of things the police could hammer and misinterpret and do wonders with."

"And that Power may already be in possession of."

"May. May not."

A lock of her ragged hair lay against his palm; he closed his fingers over it. "If Power has a club," he said in measured tones, "I have got to know what it is and where it's coming from, Karen. There's the danger—not knowing all the facts. Can't you see that?"

"Yes."

"Then why won't you be frank with me?"

"I will," Karen said.

It was like miscounting a series of familiar steps in the dark, and coming down hard on the level, on a step that wasn't there. It jolted his teeth.

It must have jolted hers as well. She goggled at him. "I *will?*"

When he'd regained his balance, Blixen said: "You know, I believe that what you did there might have been a little dog paddle."

"I believe I must be on tilt!"

Hurrying, he said: "Why did Sophocles come to see you that night?"

She returned her troubled gaze to the ceiling. "Boy, this water's deep," she said.

"Come on—"

"He—" She broke off to clear her throat. "He dropped by to ask me to sleep with him. His own words weren't quite that elegant—"

"Sophocles asked—!"

"I warned you," Karen said.

"Well, why in the name of reason would Sophocles ever assume that you—!"

"Because I'd already promised I would," Karen said.

Blixen's banished headache stirred and fluttered. He said: "Karen—"

Irritably she responded: "Look, will you please let me tell it my way? Every time you ask a question you throw me off. Let me take it at my own pace. Please. I'll get there."

"Go," Blixen said.

She spent a sulky moment gathering her mental threads, and then she sat up and hooked her arms around her calves and pressed her chin to her knees. "This was nineteen-fifty, remember," she said. "What was the worst thing about the fifties, in your judgment?"

"Korea."

"Worse yet."

"*Worse* than Korea?"

"In our family," Karen said, "the worst thing was McCarthyism."

"Ah," Blixen agreed. "And you were liberals."

"No, what we were," Karen said, "were Communists."

It occurred to Blixen that he must be getting used to the jolts; this time his teeth went virtually unrattled. "Were you, indeed," he said.

Karen nodded against her knees. "One hundred percent, died-in-the-wool Reds. My mom and my dad were, anyway. The whole thing embarrassed me. All the passion and the Spanish Loyalist recordings and the breast-beating. But it was a very large part of my dad's life. He loved the hidden commitments and the cryptograms. He loved being secretive. Maybe he never trusted anyone either, I don't know. What I do know is that the minute he thought he'd been exposed, he killed himself. I'm sure he saw suicide as his noblest gesture. He probably expected everyone to hum Puccini and weep buckets. Well, what he got—out of me at least—was a string of curses that would have made a rock star blush. I would have spit on him if my mouth hadn't been so dry."

"You say he thought he'd been exposed—"

"Because like an idiot I told him what Sophocles had told me."

"Which was what?"

"Which was that Sophocles had found a draft of a letter somewhere—I suppose in our garbage—signed by my dad, bellyaching about the cream puffs in the Party. Pop wrote that here he'd been waiting for the revolution for twenty years and all the Central Committee ever did was sit around and break wind and dream about the old days. To move everybody off their duffs, he appended a plan to assassinate Senator McCarthy."

"Your father actually—!"

Exhausted, Karen said: "Oh, Nils, this man couldn't have assassinated a chicken for Sunday dinner! He was indulging himself. He was daydreaming revolution the way other men daydream nohitters. But the school board and the neighbors and Senator McCarthy would never have understood that."

"By the way, why did Sophocles approach *you?* Why not go to your dad?"

"I suppose he thought my legs were better."

"Your body for the document?"

"Exactly."

"And all of this happened—when?"

"This happened the day before graduation. I told him I'd have to think it over. He said he'd check with me on Saturday."

"So the Friday attack—the attempted rape at Coco's party—that was a matter of his jumping the gun a little?"

"Yes. And the capper—the really unbalanced part of the whole business—was that he realized he'd committed a dreadful faux pas. He was terribly ashamed of himself. That's why he came to the house that night. To grovel and apologize. He said he'd had a beer and lost control. He promised he wouldn't lay another finger on me until Saturday. We'd make love, he said—he used those actual words—and we'd burn the letter together afterward." Pausing, Karen gnawed on her knee. "Then he reminded me that Saturday began at midnight. He said he didn't want to rush me, though, so why didn't we meet in the DeForrest gazebo between one and one-thirty? I said, in the DeForrest *gazebo?* and he said, yeah, he'd always dreamed of having a woman in the DeForrest gazebo, in front of God and the whole East Side. He said that the danger of somebody stumbling over us ought to add a little pepper to the chili. I called him a naughty boy, and said I'd meet him at one o'clock."

"But you intended to stand him up—"

"I didn't intend anything of the sort," Karen said. She clasped her knees a little closer. "What I intended," she said, "was to kill him."

Blixen studied her profile.

"You're certainly quiet," Karen said.

"How did you intend to kill him?"

"Well, I wasn't too clear about that. I figured I was stronger than he was, so I thought I'd grab a rock and bash his head in. I'd snatch the letter and make my getaway."

"What if you'd only stunned him?"

"I planned to wait until he got his clothes off and then he wouldn't have been able to chase me."

"There were no clothes in the grave," Power says. "Conjures up a curious picture, doesn't it? Now what do you suppose that ugly Greek gardener was doing out there in the buff?"

"Fortunately," Karen went on, "you blew everything sky-high when you came calling. One hour with you and I was too pooped to murder. Nothing for it but to climb to my loft and moon at the moon." After a moment she added: "Or maybe I'm not being honest. Maybe I never could have found the courage to kill him."

"In any event," Blixen said, "you scrubbed the appointment. . . . Did you leave the house at all after you came down from the loft?"

"No."

"Not even to search around the yard for me?"

"I said no." She directed an annoyed, uneasy look at him.

"Weren't you concerned about what Sophocles might do?"

"I was worried sick. I expected him to come roaring over, and when he didn't, I kept waiting for the FBI to show up. I finally got so jumpy that my dad asked me what was wrong. And I told him."

Blixen lifted his hand, cupped the beautiful skull.

Without a word, Karen lowered her knees and returned to the crook of his arm. "And that," she concluded starkly, "was the very last time I confided in anyone, or trusted anyone. Until now."

"You're swimming like a regular fish," Blixen said.

"I don't feel like a fish," Karen said. "I feel like a dumb kid who's going down for the third time because she let go of the side of the tank. I don't think you believe my story."

"You're wrong."

She allowed him to caress her skull for a while and then she said: "Anyway, along about August, I decide that Sophocles must have had second thoughts, or had panicked or something, because no one had seen hide nor hair of him since the night of the party.

But it was years before I could answer the phone without expecting to hear that smarmy voice. I used to think, Karen, you gutless wonder, you wouldn't be going through all this if you'd killed him when you had the chance. To which Power, I suppose, would say: 'Karen, you rotten liar, you *did* kill him.' Especially if the good sergeant knew about the blackmail attempt."

Blixen said: "Well, he may already know."

Karen raised her head. "How could he?"

"Through John MacVicar. John kept hinting to me that you had a sounder motive for killing Sophocles than anybody realized. He suggested that it may have had something to do with your dad."

Karen stared at him. "But—how—"

"He and Mick made a heroin buy that night. Sophocles may have run off a little at the mouth—about the date you'd made with him—and why."

"But wouldn't John have said something to me about it at the time?"

"He might have—if your dad hadn't killed himself. Maybe he figured you'd had grief enough for one summer. And also he wasn't aware that Sophocles had been stabbed. Until the skeleton was dug up."

Karen eased back onto Blixen's arm. "And you think John has already told all this to Conrad Power?"

"Hinted," Blixen said. "Hinted. Given him a glimmer. I think if it was more than a glimmer, Power would have arrested you by now."

"Bound to have," Karen whispered. "What am I going to do, Nils?"

"Relax."

"That's what I love about you, your practical suggestions."

"You'd rather panic?"

"What I'd *rather* do is hop a fast freight to Brazil."

"What, and miss all the fun when I bring the true murderer to book?"

She lay still for a moment. Then she brushed her chin absently along his bicep. "Nils—suppose you're never able to do that. I mean—it was thirty years ago. There can't be any clues left—"

"There was a witness."

"You? But suppose you never remember the face of the person with the shovel. . . . Or—suppose you remember it wrong. I mean, memory can play some funny tricks. What if you decide that I did leave the house that night—that I must have—and that it was my face behind the shovel. . . ."

"I wouldn't."

"But suppose you did." Her eyes were intent, unblinking. "I've really opened up for you tonight. I've put my life in your hands. If you decide that I killed Sophocles—would you throw me to the wolves?"

"You're not dog-paddling now, little swimmer, you're flailing. Take my hand. Stretch out. You couldn't be safer."

"I notice you haven't answered my question."

"I wouldn't throw you to the wolves," Blixen said, and bent to kiss the mouth that was raised to his.

CHAPTER EIGHT

The Heart and Soul and
Crux of the Case

I

He is not precisely dreaming.

It would be more accurate, he thinks, to say that his mind has become disengaged somehow and has ascended like a balloon to bob against the ceiling. He is both in Karen's bed and an observer of himself there. Although he lies on his left side, and the dresser is behind him, he can see every separate bead of sweat on Francina Blankers-Koen's straining face. He is spent, sated, numbed by love. He throws his right leg out. His toes explore, but find only sheet. He sits bolt upright. He is alone. He cries: "Karen!"

"Yes, darling."

She came to the bathroom door with the handle of a Hilton guest toothbrush sticking out of her mouth and soap on her nose.

His scrambled brain labored to make sense of it. "Were you in your loft?"

She had again put on her STASSEN FOR PRESIDENT sweat shirt and her warm-up pants. She smiled sadly at him around the toothbrush handle and waited for him to realize where he was.

He knew that there was no picture of Francina Blankers-Koen on the dresser, but he sneaked a look behind him anyway, and there was not. He closed his eyes and massaged his neck and said: "Wow."

"Are you back?"

"Almost."

"I'll be through in here soon and then you can shave," she said and reentered the bathroom.

But he was not ready to part with the past. He kneaded his neck muscles and tried to stay for a bit longer in that other bed under the girlish dotted swiss curtains. Something cryptic had happened in that bed in his dream, but at the same time something so grotesque that his memory preferred to rebury it rather than to accept it. He had learned to his cost not to hector a skittish memory. Bullying would only send it diving away. What was needed was casual inattention. Empty the lungs. Regulate the breathing. Slow the pulse. Return to the ceiling. Float and bob, watch and wait.

Although he lies on his left side, and the dresser is behind him, he can see every separate bead of sweat on Francina Blankers-Koen's straining face. Somehow the dream has given him lizard's eyes; they must operate independently because he can see ahead and to the sides as well as behind. Ahead is a Rand-McNally map of the world tacked to the wall beside a closet door. The door is wide open; it hides some of the map. There is a shelf of books farther along, but he cannot decipher the titles. He refocuses on the dresser. Beside Francina Blankers-Koen is a silver-backed brush, a large alarm clock indicating five minutes to one, and three small bottles, probably perfume. At the end of the cloth runner there is one more item. It seems to be a dwarf or a gnome. It wears a tall yellow hat on its pointed head, and scarlet knickers out of which stick a pair of spindly legs. Blixen cannot locate its arms. This frets him, but little by little the conviction begins to grow that he is wasting his time, that gnomes and perfume bottles and Francina Blankers-Koen have nothing to do with the problem, that he is literally looking in the wrong direction. His neck hairs prickle. He returns his attention to the closet. And he understands beyond the shadow of a doubt that this is where the secret lies. In the closet. The open closet. That wide-open—

"Next," Karen said in his ear, and kissed his temple.

The closet dove away.

"I'm not a bit hungry, Nils, but shall I order something for you while you're shaving? Eggs?"

He opened his eyes.

She was at the bedroom window, drawing the curtains; her auburn hair flamed in the sunshine.

Torpidly he thought about the lick of the flame, the sunshine—

and sat up all of a sudden and said: "It's stopped raining! When did that happen?"

"Oh, a little while ago."

He clambered out of bed and struggled into his robe and slippers and went flapping across the room to her. Below him, the Willamette bridges cast shadows again. The air had taken on a crisp, apple-smack look; toward the north and the east, the old Indian mountains—Hood, Adams, Rainier, truncated St. Helens—seemed near enough to touch. Pigeons strutted on the balcony. In the clouds blue cracks widened by the minute. "My God," Blixen breathed. "October."

Karen glanced at him. "You sound impressed."

"Aren't you?"

She returned her gaze to the mountains. "Maybe you take it more seriously than I do."

She had not bothered to put on makeup this time. Her lips were pale, her eyes lusterless.

Blixen drew her close.

"Oh, I'm all right," she told him. "I'm just aggravated with that fool Eliot. Him and his Aprils. October's the cruellest month. Look at it. All bombast and promises. Leave your house plants outside one more day, it says, and then it freezes them." Her eyes brooded over the drying city. "I'd better get going," she said, "before the next storm hits." She touched her fingertips to his lips. "Goodbye, sweet. Why are you frowning?"

"Well—I just don't see how you can stand to waste this weather. . . . All right—look, you go on about your business—eat something—drop in on Chaplin and Gogarty—"

"That's one duty I can skip. We're closed on Saturdays."

"Eat something then, and change your clothes, and I'll rent a convertible and pick you up in an hour. We'll take a ride and after that I'll drive you to Lucille's big reunion—"

"In a convertible? We'd drown." She tracked her warm-up jacket to a bench at the foot of the bed and retrieved it. "Darling, thanks so much for the invitation, but I have a thousand things on my mind. I want to wash my hair, and—oh, a thousand things—"

Her smile was cheerful and brainless, an actress's smile. The truth, Blixen suspected, was that she was already miles away, fingering complex plans like a shopper at a remnants counter. "Incidentally," she said, "I believe I'll take a rain check on Lucille's party, too. It's this tickle in my throat. As sure as God made little green apples I'm coming down with something. I'll call Lucille and explain. Well—"

"Karen," Blixen said.

"What, sweetheart?"

"Sit down."

Her eyebrows flew upward. "Nils," she said, "if you think I'm kidding about the tickle, I'm not. My whole nose is already clogged up. I can hardly smell a thing."

"Not even those burning bridges behind you?"

"What bur—? Oh, that's cute."

"It wasn't meant to be cute. Please sit down."

"Nils—!"

"Please."

Scowling, perverse, she ignored the chair he proffered and dropped onto the end of the bed.

"Now to begin with," Blixen said, "the point to consider about burning bridges isn't the blaze they make, it's the opportunity they afford. You no longer have to worry about the badlands you left because you can't return to them anyway. You've made a commitment. You've decided to trust another human being for once, to interact a little. Would you honestly rather go it alone again?"

"Yes."

"You would not."

"As usual you know more about me than I do."

"I don't, but as usual the idea that I might scares the bejesus out of you."

She surged to her feet and pointed a finger at him and opened her mouth, but closed it again without speaking and strode to the window and stared at the pigeons.

"How's the tickle?" Blixen asked.

"Go to hell."

"Will you come for a ride with me?"

"No."

"Why not?"

"Because I could just kill you. I want to take a long, hot bath and think about things."

"After the bath—"

"After the bath I intend to fix myself a bowl of chicken soup and read Proust."

"Come to the party at least."

She hunched her shoulders. "Nils, I don't want to see those people! In *particular* I don't want to have to smile and smile at that rotten SOB, Johnny MacVicar." Explosively she pivoted. "Why would he do this to me? I mean, even if Sophocles did tell him about our date, and about the blackmail and everything, why would Johnny believe him? Why pass hearsay like that along to the police when—"

"He hasn't. He hasn't yet anyway. Power would have been down on you like a ton of bricks if he had."

"Yeah, that's true. . . ." Little by little her glare dimmed. "But in that case," she went on, "what's Johnny's game? Why doesn't he let the guillotine drop? Or is that the joy of it? Hold the blade up and watch the lady squirm?"

"But he doesn't know the lady's squirming."

"Oh, he knows. That's why he told you all that stuff. He meant to upset you—so that you'd warn me."

She put a good deal of sullen bite into the words, but when Blixen grinned, she caught a glimpse of his reflection in the windowpane and grinned back at him.

"Okay, when I'm threatened, I overreact," she said. "Our Johnny's a dear, sweet boy who'd cut off his right arm before he'd hurt little old innocent me." She placed her hands on Blixen's shoulders and kissed his mouth. "Anyhow, goodbye again. After my bath, maybe I'll make a MacVicar doll and stick pins into it and foil all his evil designs. If I change my mind about Lucille's party, I'll phone you, but don't hold your breath. I'm sorry we couldn't get any forrader with the Case of the Butchered Skeleton. But we did have fun, didn't we?"

"Oh," Blixen said, "speaking of forrader—"

She paused inquiringly at the door.

"Karen—that bedroom closet of yours . . . Why was it open?"

"When, darling? The night we were together? Is it important?"

"Yes."

"Why?"

"I don't know."

She had bent forward as though she had gone a little deaf, or he'd begun to speak in a foreign language, and she needed to make certain of every word. "Right," she said vaguely, and eased back. "Well, let me see. I know I was wearing my robe in the loft because I was cold and I remember buttoning the collar. Which means that I probably went into the closet to get it. Yes, I must have. I'm pretty sure I did."

"Nothing out of the way in there?"

"Like what?"

What shone? Fire? Jewelry? "No odd lights of any kind?"

"There was one dim little bulb I might have switched on. Do you mean like that?"

He concentrated on the glow. "Where was this bulb located?"

"Right inside the door. It was a jerry-built thing that my dad rigged up. Six miles of splices and a double socket that hissed when you bumped it. It hung down from a hook in the ceiling."

"And you bumped it that night when you went in?"

"Did I? I don't know. I thought I'd learned to duck under it by then."

"I can see it twitch and shiver. . . . Something brushed against it. . . ."

"Ghosts," Karen said.

He glanced up to catch her smiling at him.

"Well, darling, excuse me," she laughed, "but you look so solemn. You'd think that that one lousy little light bulb was the heart and soul and crux of the whole—"

"Case?" Blixen finished, and studied her for the space of a double heartbeat, and said: "Yes. I believe it is."

II

But if he knew in his bones it was the crux, he still could not say why it was, nor what its ramifications might be, nor whom it incriminated. The face behind the shovel remained intransigently vague.

After Karen jogged off, he put the whole thing out of his mind. He cut himself shaving.

He ordered an enormous breakfast, sampled it joylessly, and opted instead for a walk down Broadway, past the gap-toothed space where the majestic old Portland Hotel had been, around a number of the short blocks he'd trod as a child. He stopped for a drink at one of Simon Benson's public water fountains. He located a United Airlines ticket office, and requested a reservation on the Sunday flight to Honolulu. While his American Express card was being processed, he fell into a brown study over a half-open doorway behind the clerk.

"Sir," she said.

She had said it a number of times, he suspected, and he forced his eyes around to hers and replied: "I'm sorry! My mind was—I was thinking about your storeroom there."

She continued to extend the credit card charge slip toward him.

"Even with the light on like that," Blixen said, "it's impossible to see more than a foot or two inside, isn't it." He could feel his face growing pink. He bent over the credit card slip. "Yes—by the X? There. Thank you—"

"Thank *you*," said the clerk. She handed him his ticket and his receipt and transferred her attention to the next customer.

But when Blixen glanced back from the door, he surprised her watching him. They each smiled and looked aside.

III

All the same, the image of the dark storeroom remained like a burr at the edge of his mind as he wool-gathered his way down Morrison Street and then northward along a mall studded with bus kiosks and weathered sculptures.

The bright breezy weather, it seemed to him, had coaxed an unusual number of eccentrics outdoors. Evangelists simpered and offered him tracts. Kids skated past balancing stereos the size of trunks on their shoulders. Beside a handcart, a chap in a braided pigtail chalked prices for hot sandwiches on a child's blackboard and sang Schubert sotto voce.

Blixen had traveled nearly forty feet farther before the words on the menu hit him.

He slowed, stopped.

Breasting the tide, he made his way back to the handcart.

"You're next, ace," said the pigtailed chap.

Blixen indicated the menu. "Tell me," he said, "what exactly is a Dracula Dog?"

"How do I explain thee, let me count the ways. That there's a dead wiener in a coffin bun, smothered under special blood sauce, with a toothpick stake driven straight through its little heart. Delicious."

"But of course you must remain," insists the count in his liquid, red-lipped way. "It's true that I'm not prepared for guests, but I could make up a nice grave in the basement."

"Plus just a soupçon of garlic," said the man in the pigtail, "for safety's sake."

Out of his coffin rises the count, eyes wide and dead, flashlight in mouth, cheeks glowing—

But that was absurd, Blixen thought irritably. What was his subconscious attempting to suggest? That Chaplin the trickster had been crouched that night in his own daughter's closet? To frighten them? Spy on them? Preposterous. Chaplin had been unpredictable, not sick.

"How about a Frankensteinfurter?" suggested the pigtailed man. "Electrically resurrected at the very height of last night's storm."

"Mouth-watering," Blixen said. "The Lincoln Tower. How far away would that be?"

"Oh—six blocks, seven blocks. You go up here to—"

"Thanks. I'll find a phone."

He wheeled, bumped into a unisexual person in an ankle-length raincoat, and apologized over his shoulder all the way to a nearby variety store. The pay booths were located toward the rear of the building, in ladies' nightgowns. He dialed Karen's number from memory, and then decided after four rings that he must have transposed a digit somewhere, but before he could hang up, she said: "Hello?"

"Yes, Karen, hi—Nils," Blixen said hurriedly. "Karen—"

"Hoo-hoo, she's not here," interrupted the voice on the phone. "Hello?" Blixen said.

"This is Helen the housekeeper," said the voice. "Miz Chaplin's out. I haven't seen her all day. Can I take a message?"

"You mean—she didn't show up for lunch? Chicken soup? Or a bath?"

"Say, who *is* this?" demanded Helen the housekeeper.

"A friend—"

Ominously Helen the housekeeper said: "Friend, I think you better give me your name."

"Ah," Blixen said. "All right, tell her Nils Blixen called."

"Bill what?"

"Never mind," Blixen muttered. "Thank you."

He broke the connection, and remained unmoving in the booth, one hand on the dead receiver, gazing into space.

IV

He believed he could hear the phone in his suite ringing as he emerged from the elevator, but by the time he had fumbled his way through the door, the sound had stopped. He headed for the bathroom, but circled back when the ringing recommenced.

He lifted the receiver. "Blixen."

"Now that," Karen said, "is what I call businesslike." She lowered her voice a plummy notch. "Afternoon, Blixen, Chaplin here. Want to go out and ruin some widows and orphans?"

"Well, you sound mighty manic all of a sudden."

"I do and I am. It's this *dazzling* day. I wish now I'd let you take me on that ride. Did you have fun?"

"I walked."

"Even better. You didn't also happen to call me a while ago, did you? My housekeeper said some degenerate phoned and breathed at her and said his name was Bill. Right away I figured it must have been you. Was it?"

"Yeah."

"I'm so sad I missed you. I just got back from my own walk."

Blixen glanced at his watch. "You walked from eleven o'clock to half-past four?"

"No, I walked from about four to about four-twenty. The rest of the time I sat in my store and played with the puppies, fed the snakes, one thing and another."

"How did I gain the impression that your shop was closed on Saturdays?"

"Because I told you it was. And it is. But sometimes I—" The words died away. "Nils?" she resumed. "Am I being grilled or something?"

Beside the Dresden shepherdess lay a beheaded peanut. The

maids hadn't yet been in to clean. Blixen leaned his forehead on his hand and sensed her presence like perfume throughout the whole, sunny, disarranged suite and missed her. "Maybe you are," he said. "Either I'm confused or I'm jealous. You talk to me about chicken soup and Proust, but you go to Gogarty."

"Gogarty! *Me?* Have you cracked *up?* I can't even laugh at that it's so crazy! I wouldn't have set foot in the place if Gogarty had been there! Didn't I tell you how much I—all right, enough of this. Here's what happened. I *meant* to go home, but the minute I hit the street I remembered that this was Helen's day to clean and I realized I wasn't in shape to help or talk or anything else. All I wanted to do was try to get my soul together. So I detoured down to Fourth and unlocked the shop and went in and walked around and cried and thought—"

"Cried?"

"A little, not much. And when I felt better I saw it was almost four so I came on home. Tell me again you're jealous. Or was it only confusion after all?"

"No, it was jealousy."

"That makes me so happy I could scream. Better hold your ear away from the phone."

Marveling, Blixen said: "I just can't believe this is the same doomed woman who trudged out of here this morning muttering about chicken soup."

"It isn't, that's why. That's what comes of working things through. Now I love the whole world."

"Even John MacVicar?"

"You sure are adept at stamping on a person's spiritual toes, aren't you, Blixen?"

"Three-time national singles champion," Blixen said. "But, look, there's no need to worry about it, we've—"

"Don't crowd me, I'm thinking," Karen said. "Very well. Let me be honest. I do not love the whole world." She hesitated, and then added in a strange tone: "But at least I'm not afraid of John anymore."

"Good! Unafraid enough to come with me to Lucille's party after all?"

This time her hesitation was much shorter, her voice far more crisp. "All right. Why not? Yes. It'll be fun. I'll see you and your snappy convertible at six-thirty. You won't have to come up. I'll meet you out front. By the way, this earlier call of yours—what was that about?"

Red-cheeked, the count rises out of his casket. . . .

"Oh, your closet," he said. "I got to thinking about your closet again—wondering how deep it was—"

"You know the term 'closet' may have thrown you off, Nils. It wasn't deep at all. Not much bigger than a tall cupboard, really."

"Deep enough to dress in?"

"Not unless you were a Lilliputian. It was—um—maybe eighteen inches front to back—say three feet wide—"

Presently Blixen said: "What about extra access? Any connecting doors?"

"Nils, it was a narrow, dumpy, inconvenient little hole-in-the-wall! A *closet!* No sliding panels, no priest-holes, no nothing! Why do you keep fussing over it?"

"I wish I knew," Blixen said. And then thought about it and added, half to himself: "I think I wish I knew. . . ."

CHAPTER NINE

Reunion

I

Because Hertz couldn't offer him a convertible, Blixen turned to Avis, which couldn't offer him one either. In the end he found a Cadillac equipped with a sunroof at National, and accepted that. As a bonus, the car was able to play "Blue Tango" on one of its horns, so he came swooping up to the Lincoln Tower entrance beating time to Blue Tango through his sunroof. True to her word, Karen was out front, but she refused to join him until he stopped his languorous racket because she said she had her reputation to think of.

She never had looked lovelier, although Blixen would have been the first to admit that it was a clear case of the model rising above her material. Under an ankle-length coat of some unknown whitish fur she wore bleached jeans and what appeared to be a gypsy violinist's shirt. She had pulled a woolen stocking-cap over her ears. She sat near the passenger window with her hands clenched under her armpits and asked Blixen to close the sunroof. She said she was cold as ice.

"Closed it shall be," Blixen intoned, "and closed it shall remain. And may I add, my dear, that you look ravishing tonight?"

"Sure, mock," she said.

Her voice sounded so careworn that he glanced at her in surprise.

"Nils, don't *stare* at me! Watch the road. You'll kill us both." Moodily she gazed out the window. "Which might be preferable at that to spending an entire evening with those screwed-up, bloodthirsty friends of yours—"

"Bloodthirsty?"

"You heard me, bloodthirsty. Every single one of them is absolutely dying for the cops to arrest me. I can hear it in their voices. Everybody thinks I murdered Sophocles."

"Not me."

"Yes, but you don't count." She straightened, aghast. "I mean, of course you count, but you're so prejudiced it throws the whole balance off. But you *count*—" Contritely she pressed as close to him as the seats allowed, and he raised his right arm to embrace her and brought it up and across her left forearm and felt her shudder in pain and heard her groan against his chin.

He said: "Karen, what did I do—?"

"Nothing—"

"Is it your arm? Let me see—pull your sleeve up—"

"Will you please—oh, good grief." With the poorest possible grace, she pushed back her coat sleeve and fussed over the two mother-of-pearl buttons at the wrist of her gypsy violinist's shirt. "You'd think I was some—there! Now are you happy?"

He glanced at the forearm she'd thrust in front of him. A blood-red scratch scored the soft skin from elbow almost to palm. She had dabbed iodine on the parts that had been torn the deepest. The backs of his thighs twitched in compassion. "Well, how in the—" he began.

"One of the cats scratched me. It happens all the time. I'm covered with scratches."

"I don't remember seeing any."

"Well, they're there." She pointed ahead. "Lucille and Clem live at the edge of Ladd's Addition. Go down Twentieth." She drew away from him, and rebuttoned her sleeve and sat morosely against her own window for the rest of the trip.

II

There were two cars parked in front of Clem and Lucille's house—Clem's battered Datsun, and a rust-spotted yellow Buick—so Blixen pulled into the driveway and honked at Lucille, who was smoking a cigarette on the front stoop and looking the other way. Lucille gave a convulsive lurch and wheeled like a battleship coming into line, but dropped her scowl at once when she saw who it was. Arms wide, she rushed down the steps. "Nils—!"

Chuckling, Blixen climbed out of the car and into her pillowy hug. She had expanded; he could think of no other word for it. The space between her cheekbones was wider; her hips and shoulders strained the seams of a tentlike caftan. "Oh, Nils, Nils, *Nils,*" she cried, "if you aren't a sight for sore eyes!"

"What am I, just a sight?" Karen asked. She emerged from the car in sections, her attention fixed on the house.

"Well, ducks," Lucille crooned, "you're a sight for sore eyes, too. . . ." She gripped Karen's ears and planted a kiss on the top of her stocking-cap. She extended her arms, frowning. "Are you sick? You look bleached out." To Blixen she said: "Come to think of it, you both seem a little pale. Where'd you get the black eye?"

"Zigged when he should have zagged," Karen said. She pried herself free. "Don't tell me we're the first—"

"You're the middle," said Lucille. "Coco and Agnes are here, but who knows when Johnny'll come pooping in. I never knew a doctor in my life to be on time."

"Maybe he won't come at all."

"Listen, Johnny MacVicar'll show up if he has to crawl. He's nuts about my soup. He can't chew, so I made him a special—are you shaking?"

"No," Karen said.

"Why, you are, too, look at you!"

"Dear," Karen said through clenched teeth, and then grimaced at Blixen. "Nils, I'll see you inside, okay? I'm frozen stiff." She waved and buried her chin in her collar and ran across the lawn and up the steps into the house.

Lucille heaved herself about to inspect Blixen. "Frozen?" she said.

"There are chillier winds in heaven and earth, Horatio," Blixen mused, "than are dreamt of in your philosophy."

After a time Lucille said: "You mean that's a tension chill."

"I think it might be."

Lucille gazed back at the slammed door. "Well, she's got her reasons. . . . If I were God, Nils, I'd see that Conrad Power burned in hell for scaring her like this. Clem thinks he must have terminal softening of the brain." The ash on her cigarette collapsed: She slapped at it, blew it off her chest. "Oh, this filthy habit," she snarled. "Are you frozen, too, or can you wait until I finish here? I don't dare smoke in the house. Clem just raises cain."

"*Clem* does?"

"Can you believe that? Yeah, old three-packs-a-day Gompers quit six weeks ago and now he's holier than a Catholic convert. Drives me nuts." She puffed gloomily. "Although I think he sneaks one now and again. I smell it on him. Did he have any last night?"

"Not while he was with me."

"I wondered because he seemed so jumpy when he came home. Pace, pace, pace, back and forth. He kept me up until half-past three." She examined her cigarette, took one final drag on it, and pitched the stub into the street. "He wanted me to cancel the party tonight," she said.

"Really? Why?"

"He can't stand John MacVicar, for one thing. But he seemed to be mostly worried about Karen. He said it wouldn't be fair to her, that we'd all sit around and try to make small talk and how do you talk small to somebody who's apt to be picked up any minute for murder?"

"Why can't he stand Johnny?"

Lucille sighed. "Oh, Nils, maybe that's too strong a word for it. He can *stand* him, it's just—well, John gets on Clemmie's nerves. All that Freudian jargon. I mean, my heavens, you remember what an ass John was as a boy. The Alfred E. Neuman of Alameda Ridge. Mickey at least had a certain low cunning. But John? Saints preserve us. And yet all of a sudden here he is the wise old shrink treating half the nuts in the Northwest. Clem thinks he's a terrible phoney."

Blixen crossed his arms, leaned back against the Cadillac. "Lucille, how well did you know John and Mick when we were kids?"

"I wouldn't say we were *intimate*—"

"But you could tell them apart?"

"Oh, definitely."

"And you're quite sure it was Mick you saw in the Hamburger Hut on the night of the murder? I ask because John claims you were mistaken—that he was the one you ran into. He says he came into the Hut alone to talk to Sophocles."

"And that was *John?* Huh." Lucille searched her bosom for something, perhaps cigarettes. "Well, he ought to know." Decisively she abandoned the bosom. "No, damn it, I'm right! That was Mick, and I'll tell you why! His nosebleed! You remember those terrible nosebleeds Mickey used to get—well, Clem and I were at the counter and in walks this bloody apparition, and Clemmie goes, 'Mick! My gosh, what did you do, run into a buzz saw?' and Mick says no, it was just a nosebleed. Well I had a handkerchief in my pocket, and I started to offer it to him, but Clemmie stopped me, you know, and he says, 'What are you, crazy? Your dumb mother'll think I raped you or something.' So we wiped Mick off with paper napkins!" She stared at Blixen in triumph. "Oh, that was Mick all right," she said. "Listen, I knew Mick MacVicar when I saw him."

"So," Blixen began, "if—"

"Wait a second, there's Clem, we'll ask Clem," Lucille said and waved past Blixen toward the front door. "Honey!"

"Hey, amigo!" Gompers yelled thinly from the house. Neckless as a hippo he stood behind the screen in a polo shirt and Bermuda shorts and beamed out at them. "Come on, professor, you're holding up the party! What are you trying to do out there, seduce my wife?"

"Terrific," Lucille snorted. But the compliment had tickled her. Blushing, she led the way across the lawn.

Gompers held the screen door open for them, pumped Blixen's hand, guffawing through his big mustache. "Hey, I see you escaped! Congratulations! The last time I saw this poor soul, Lucille, he was being hauled off by the police." He'd drawn Blixen into a lighted entryway; now he tilted forward in sudden surprise. "Jesus, your eye," he said. "What did they do, give you the third degree?"

"Darling," Lucille informed her husband, "I think we're supposed to be frightfully discreet and pretend not to notice it. My own theory is that he tried to get fresh with Karen on the way over here and she socked him."

Gompers jumped. "Karen. I knew there was something I wanted to—" He lowered his voice. "It's that damned Agnes, Babe. The first thing she said when Karen walked in was 'Oh, good, you're still loose,' so Karen marched straight on into the kitchen and I think she's crying."

"Well, why didn't you—" Lucille began, and then snapped: "God, men—" and hurried off.

"All my fault, as always," Gompers said. He puffed out his mustache. "Gonna be a looooong night, pardner. I begged Lucille to cancel this thing and just have you over alone, but oh, no . . ." He brightened. "Well, thank God for booze. What can I build you? Scotch? Go on in and sit down. I'll be right back."

There was an enormous living room to the left, a player piano in a corner, a tall artificial Christmas tree in the bay window, a long sofa and three easy chairs grouped around a crackling fireplace. In one of the easy chairs, a powdered old lady perked up and extended her bony hands to Blixen. "Nils! You're older—"

Gallantly Blixen said: "But you aren't, Mrs.—"

"It's still Miss, believe it or not. And call me Coco, for heaven's sake."

"Coco, right," Blixen said. His gums had dried; his lips felt frozen in a permanent smirk.

The skeletal fingers trembled in his. "Mom and I watch your program every week. You're the neighborhood celebrity." She patted the chair beside her. "Sit down and tell me all about Hollywood. Whatever happened to George Nader?"

But before Blixen could reply, a tall, white-haired woman in an orange gown entered the living room from the hall and Coco cried: "Oh, Mama, look who's here! You remember our celebrity, don't you?"

"No," said Mrs. DeForrest.

From the kitchen, Gompers shouted: "Nils, did you say scotch?"

"Please!"

"Your toilet's stuck," shouted Mrs. DeForrest.

Rattled, Gompers bumped the swinging kitchen door open. "*Again?*" He backed out of the kitchen with a drink in each hand and made his way to Blixen. "Scotch for this gentleman—Bourbon for the host. . . ." He glanced warily at the women. "Are you sure I can't fetch you ladies a little something? Orange juice? Coke? No? Nothing?"

Catching Gompers's eye, Blixen said: "How's—?" and nodded toward the kitchen.

Gompers nodded. "Better. Somewhat." He forced a smile, lifted his glass. "Health, Nils."

"Who's better?" Mrs. DeForrest asked.

"Oh . . ." Gompers said foggily, and sipped at his drink. "Was I supposed to do something?" he asked.

"Fix the toilet," said Mrs. DeForrest.

"Damn! Yes!" Gompers cried, and parked his drink on the table. "Nils, excuse me. Talk to the girls. Talk about TV. Nils produces 'Trapper John,'" Gompers called over his shoulder and vanished down the hall.

Blixen said: "He means 'Stagg at Bay.' Nice to see you again, Mrs. DeForrest. It's been a while."

Gimlet-eyed, Mrs. DeForrest settled back on the sofa. "Well, which one is it, 'Trapper John' or 'Stagg at Bay'?"

"It's 'Stagg at Bay.'"

"Biggest bore on the tube," said Mrs. DeForrest. "Now 'Trapper John' is fun. I like 'Jackpot.'"

"That's it," Coco muttered, and floundered to her feet. "Don't get up," she said unnecessarily to Blixen. "I'll just see if I can help in the kitchen." She trotted off, high heels clacking.

When Blixen glanced back, Mrs. DeForrest grinned. "I embarrass her," she said. "I don't care. She embarrassed me more than once when she was little." She squinted at him. "Nils . . . Say, are you the one who caught me in the kitchen crying?" She waved a hand. "Oh, you wouldn't remember."

"I do remember. You told me it was the onions."

"Um." Mrs. DeForrest fell silent, heavy knees spread. Only the flame glitter in her half-open eyes indicated that she had not drifted into an elderly nap. "Well," she resumed at last, "it wasn't the onions. Which you no doubt realized. The fact is my beloved husband had just announced over the phone that he was leaving me."

"That man," Blixen murmured, "understood timing, didn't he?"

"Didn't he?" Down went the chin to the breast, the eyes to the fire. "Of course I told him I couldn't argue then, with all you kids around. He was due to fly east the next day. He was a lumber grader. Every couple of years, off he'd trot to visit his eastern mills and his floozies. Anyway, I asked him to postpone the trip so we could talk a little, but he said, no, there was nothing to discuss, he was through, period. I says, 'Well, Gil, I'll never let you have a divorce, you know that,' and he says, 'Oh, I think you will, Agnes.'" She wrapped the quote in a villain's rasp.

"It was a threat, then."

"Big threat. The old fool. I wasn't scared. When the Pope condones divorce, I'll condone it. That's the one thing Gil never could beat out of me, my Catholicism."

"Did he try? That night?" Blixen hesitated. "Or—maybe you'd rather not talk about this, Mrs. DeForrest."

"Hah," Mrs. DeForrest said, "if you can't talk about it, you can't exorcise it. That is lesson number one on how to handle being dumped." She forced herself to breathe through her nose. Her thumb pushed a golden wedding ring around and around the third finger of the left hand. "So—yes—he beat me that night. Beat me and kicked me and breezed out of my life like a blown-away dandelion. The strange part is that once I realized he was gone for good, I didn't know whether to cry or applaud. I was lost. But I was relieved, too."

"Did he ever try to contact you?"

"Twice. He sent a card on my birthday, and then he wrote from Chicago two years later to say he was down and out, and would I take him back. He said he thought he had cancer. But he wouldn't see a doctor for fear they'd operate."

"How did you react to his letter?"

"Same way I reacted to the birthday card. I didn't even show it to Coco. I tore it up and threw it on the compost heap." Around and around went the golden ring. "But then—I don't know—about —oh, a month after the letter came, Coco landed a job at Jantzen, which gave us a little breathing space, money-wise, so I said to myself, now, Agnes, come on, grow up, there was something there once, it's not going to hurt you to say goodbye—" The dronish voice wobbled, stopped. Mrs. DeForrest blinked in amazement, at the far wall. "Would you believe this?" she said. "I'm crying."

"And was he still alive when you reached him?"

"Died in my arms," said Mrs. DeForrest. She dredged a crumpled Kleenex out of the neck of her dress, and blew her nose. "Talk about East Lynne. I asked for an autopsy, and sure enough, it was cancer. All through him." Mrs. DeForrest folded and re-folded the Kleenex. "The mills of God," she said.

Meditatively, Blixen said: "Mrs. DeForrest—did he leave any-thing? Any—"

"Not a plugged nickel. Well, that's not fair. He *had* kept up one little five-thousand-dollar insurance policy, but he'd borrowed al-most three thousand against it, so all they sent me was twenty-one hundred. But who's complaining? You can buy a lot of macaroni and cheese for twenty-one hundred. What I meant was that we couldn't find any cash in the room. No bankbooks, pawn tickets. Nothing. He must have sold his diamond stickpin and his jewelry box with the mirror on top, which were the only personal things he took when he left, because they weren't there either."

Blixen, searching for a scrap of paper to write on, came across the American Express card receipt in his coat pocket. He spread it on the coffee table, uncapped his pen. "Actually," he said, "what I had in mind were—oh, notes—last testaments—"

"I never found any."

"Did he realize he was dying?"

"I believe he did."

"Did he ask for a priest?"

Mrs. DeForrest planted her hands on the sofa cushion and jim-mied herself around to face him. "What's that got to do with the price of eggs?"

Blixen finished his note. He glanced up. "Mrs. DeForrest," he said, "did you know that Sophocles Kanaris was a drug pusher?"

The position Mrs. DeForrest had assumed on the sofa—the twist of her trunk, the hunch of her shoulders—had lent her an ornithoid air. She might have been a bare-headed buzzard perched in an Af-rican tree, thinking of meat.

"Mrs. DeForrest?"

"No," said Mrs. DeForrest. "Was he?"

"How did your husband feel about Sophocles?"

"Shame on you," said Mrs. DeForrest. "Who told you about that fight?"

Blixen's heart had begun to pound. "What fight?"

"Your fancy lady friend told you, didn't she," said Mrs. De-Forrest. "Karen what's-her-name. I heard about you two. She hollers for help and up you run, all full of piss and vinegar. Well, you aren't going to whitewash your woman at Gilbert DeForrest's expense, sonny boy." Blood suffused her face; a vein thumped in her neck. "He was filth. But he was my filth." The statement appeared to take her by surprise. She pressed her fingers to her throat and gazed, nonplussed, into the fire.

Blixen touched her wrist. "Ma'am, what was this fight about?"

"There was no fight."

"Drugs? Coco?"

Teeth bared, Mrs. DeForrest swung back to face him. "Yes, and what would you have done, closed your eyes to it? Clicked her purse shut and begged her pardon? I mean, there they were, dirty little pinched-in brown things! I thought they were cigarettes she'd rolled herself. I says, 'Gil, look here, your precious daughter's been smoking,' and he smells one and he says, 'Smoking, smoking, for God's sake, don't you know dope when you see it, that's marijuana!' Well, I just sat down and bawled. I says, 'Where did you find these awful things, you filthy girl!' And Gil says, 'That degenerate gardener sold 'em to her, that's where!' But she wouldn't tell. 'All right,' Gil says, 'no graduation party for you, missy, and if I catch that Greek so-and-so on my property again, I'll kill him!' "

Again the spate of words seemed to glaze Mrs. DeForrest's eyes. She paused to pat the spittle off her chin. "Just talk, though, he didn't mean any of it. Coco'd bought her a cute new outfit, and we'd made the punch and sandwiches. The party went on as scheduled."

"The party," Blixen repeated, "went on. And Sophocles showed up—"

"To work. He always came on Fridays. I informed him his services were no longer needed. But he wouldn't go. He said I'd slandered him. 'I'm no drug dealer,' he says, 'and I won't be slandered and I won't be fired without rhyme or reason.' 'Well,' I says, 'if that's your view of it, fine, but it's not Mr. DeForrest's and my view, and if I was you, sir, I'd be long gone from here by the time Mr. DeForrest walks into this yard.' And of course he was."

"And of course," Blixen said, "he returned."

Mrs. DeForrest continued to pat her chin.

"At twenty minutes to one," Blixen went on, "a policeman saw Johnny and Mick MacVicar near Thirty-eighth and Fremont.

Sophocles was in the car with them. He got out, and he started walking east, toward the bus stop at Forty-first. Twenty minutes later he was sprawled in a grave in your driveway with one of your butcher knives in his chest."

"And you're hinting what! That my husband—"

"Did Gil ask for a priest, Mrs. DeForrest?"

"Oh, if you knew how funny this was, you'd laugh! No, he never called for a *priest,* he never said one word to me or anybody else about *Sophocles,* he was—"

The door chimes sounded.

Jumping, Mrs. DeForrest sized up the hallway and then fell back. "Oh, shame on you, *shame* on you," she said.

The front knocker clanged against its iron base. The chimes pealed for a second time.

"Will somebody for sweet Jesus' sake GET that?" Clem howled from below. "Lucille, I need a plumber! Call the plumber! Answer the door!"

"Excuse me," Blixen grunted, and struggled to his feet just as Karen flew out of the kitchen waving a wet spoon and looking wild-eyed.

"There's your murderer!" cried Mrs. DeForrest.

Karen broke stride, but Blixen grabbed her elbow and said: "It's all right, little hysteria here," and hustled her toward the front door as the knocking recommenced.

He might have been pulling a child away from a mud puddle. She had locked her knees, skewed her head back. "Don't—quit *wrenching* at me! What did she say? Nils, it's time we had this out once and for all—!"

"Fine. Have it out. But let's let John in first—"

The elbow twisted, freed itself. Blixen turned, but Karen made no attempt to peel back into the living room. She seemed momentarily as inanimate as Lot's pillar of a wife. Her lips stirred. "Let who in? It can't be Johnny. I mean, Johnny wouldn't have the guts —to—" She breathed: "Oh, Nils," and moved around and past him down the hallway toward the bedrooms and the rear of the house.

Baffled, Blixen started after her, but before he had taken his second step, the chimes erupted again, and he stopped to yank the door open. "John, for God's sake—!"

But it wasn't John.

Blixen managed to catch a fractured glimpse of two dour faces —Power's, and an unfamiliar male's—and then Power had slammed him aside and was clattering down the hall, braying: "Miss Chaplin!" and Karen had become transfixed again, this time at the guest bedroom door. Power reined himself in. "Swinnerton, come on!" he shouted.

"Swinnerton!" shouted the unfamiliar man across Blixen's ear, and Officer Swinnerton—pillbox shape, Tartar eyes and all— plunged through the door past Blixen into the shadows. Expertly she wheeled Karen around. "Face the wall, feet apart, lean forward—" She whacked at the jeans pockets, patted down the legs, waist, chest, arms. Stepped back. " 'Kay," she said.

" 'Kay, thanks," Power said. He swept off his tweed cap, fished a dog-eared card out of the crown, held the card at arm's length under the hall light. "Karen Chaplin," he read, "you are under arrest. The law provides you with certain rights. Before we go on, you must understand what these rights are.

"First—"

CHAPTER TEN

You Have the Right to Remain Silent

I

"HOLD IT!" Blixen roared.

In the kitchen somebody dropped a pan.

Mrs. DeForrest, lured to the hallway by the rumpus, looked on vacantly, mouth agape.

At the end of the hallway Karen remained frozen against the wall. Her eyes were huge in the semidarkness; her pallid face swam in the shadows.

Blixen walked past Power, motioned to Karen. "Put your arms down," he said. "Come here."

Obedient as a child, Karen squeezed past Swinnerton and joined Blixen under the light.

"Give me the spoon."

She released it.

Blixen stashed it under one armpit and placed both palms on her shoulders and gazed into her eyes. "All right, our poor friend, Mr. Power," he said, "has finally flipped. He'll learn that very shortly, to his cost. In the meantime, I don't want you to say one word to him, not a word, hello, goodbye, nothing. Do you understand?"

She nodded.

"Go ahead, Power."

But before Power could focus on his card again, Coco's blank face appeared over Mrs. DeForrest's shoulder. "Mama, what's everybody—"

"They've arrested your little pal, that's what," panted Mrs. De-Forrest. "Go tell Lucille."

"Arr—" Abruptly Coco clamped both hands over her open mouth. "Oh, my *God*—"

"Oh, and Coco," Blixen said, "while you're back there, would you call Karen's attorney? His name is Duffield. Inform Mr. Duffield we'll meet him at Central Precinct in about fifteen minutes."

"Central Precinct, Central Precinct," Coco muttered mechanically, and went pitching away like a great gaunt bird through the living room on her way to the kitchen.

"Hey, shall we give old *Miranda* another go?" asked Power's associate. "Third time's the charm."

"Burkhardt," Power warned.

"I understand my rights," Karen told Blixen. "Tell him he can skip all that."

"In that case, I now hand you a waiver form," Power said. "If you're willing to answer questions without having an attorney present, just sign on line five. Will you sign the waiver?"

"No," Karen said to Blixen.

"Takes care of the waiver," said Power, and folded it irritably and stuffed it into his shirt pocket, and glowered off toward the living room as Lucille and Coco came windmilling across the carpet like a couple of bad tumblers.

"Karen, Clem's calling Duffield," Lucille was bawling, "Karen? Where's Karen?"

"Here," Karen said.

Lucille muscled her way between Power and Blixen, and snatched Karen to her bosom. Savagely she said: "Now you keep your trap shut. Don't you so much as give these people the time of day."

"She understands," Swinnerton said.

"Who the hell asked you?" Lucille shouted at her. "What are you doing here anyway! Busting doors in, harassing peaceful citizens! Why don't you go catch some real criminals! Go catch the Slasher! Go—"

"We did," Power said.

Jumping, Lucille shouted: "Did what? Who—"

"You caught the *Slasher?*" Gompers cried from behind Agnes.

He jostled Coco aside, skidded up to Blixen. "Duffield's out, I left a message," he sputtered. And to Power: "Who was it? Not Flinders—"

"It was Flinders," Power said. He smiled at Blixen. "Along with his lady friend. She broke down this afternoon. Seems God told 'em to do it. Too many drunken derelicts in the world. So much for your big mystery, Mr. B. She killed Number Five on her own while her barber-boyfriend was in the clink."

"Then she's confessed to the fifth killing?"

"Not yet. But she will."

"What was his name?" Gompers asked.

"Whose name?"

"Number Five's. The poor soul who spent those three glorious weeks in the fruit cupboard."

"John W. Smith, according to the Burnside barflies. He showed up last July. He'd bum food off the local grocers—"

Slowly Blixen said: "Power, what did you just say?"

"Eh?"

"Something doesn't fit," Blixen said. "You were talking about something, and I thought to myself: *No, that can't be true—*"

"John W. Smith?" Gompers put in.

"No . . ."

"Was it before that? The girl friend?"

"No," Blixen murmured. He stared at the floor for a second longer and then looked at Power. "Incidentally, Sergeant, tell me —how did you happen to know where to find Miss Chaplin tonight? Or—have you had a tail on her?"

Power flicked a glance at Burkhardt, returning his gaze to Blixen. "No tail, no," he said. "Which may turn out to be the worst error of judgment I ever made. As to why we're here, an informant mentioned your big reunion. Miss Chaplin failed to answer her apartment buzzer, so we thought we'd come on over." He pulled at his titanic nose. "Any more questions?"

"Yes," Blixen said. "Is Macy's ready to tell Gimbels yet?"

Power's eyes faded and then gleamed. "Ah, Macy's." Laughing, he tapped his nose with his knuckle. "Well, sure, why not," he said. "Sale's over, the profits are in. . . ." He licked his lips. "Mr. B.," he said, "we discovered her motive."

Karen shifted uneasily, but before she could open her mouth,

Blixen put a hand on her arm to quiet her and said: "Did you now, Sergeant."

"And can you guess *where* we discovered it? Of all places? Seattle."

"No kidding."

"I kid you not, Seattle," Power said. "Miss Chaplin—I wonder if you remember a man named Leopold Crossinggard. Bald-headed fellow—looked a lot like Daddy Warbucks—? No? Strange. He spent a number of weekends with you and your family in the late nineteen-forties. Well, no matter. The fact is that this Reverend Crossinggard has been an absolute godsend to the authorities lately, so when—"

"Reverend?" Karen whispered.

Even through the gypsyish shirt, Karen's skin felt clammy to Blixen.

"Born-again," Power said. "Can you credit that? His flock maintains that there hasn't been a conversion to match it since Saul went to Damascus. It seems he was flipping the TV dial one day and who should he stumble over but Jerry Falwell—"

"Power—" Blixen said.

"Admitted. I ramble. And of course you can't appreciate the enormity of the thing until you know who Crossinggard was in his *first* life. Make a guess."

"J. Edgar Hoover."

Power whooped until he wept, and even Officer Swinnerton cracked a smile.

Wearily Blixen said: "Okay, Sergeant, who exactly was Leopold Crossinggard in his first life?"

"Miss Chaplin," Power guffawed, "tell him—!"

"She doesn't remember."

"Of course she doesn't. You're right again." Power sighed and rubbed the heels of his hands across his eyes. "Well, sir," he said, "for twelve mortal years, from nineteen thirty-nine until August of nineteen fifty-one, Leopold Crossinggard was a member of the Washington State section of the Communist Party of the United States of America. And for twelve mortal years, Crossinggard corresponded almost monthly with the Coordinating Secretary of the Oregon section's Small Business Fraction, who lived at that time in Portland and went by the name of Louis Bollinger Chaplin and who was the father of our very own Miss Karen Chaplin."

"Oh, shit," Coco breathed, and hunched her shoulders up to her ears and squeezed her eyes shut when her mother threw her a look of horror. "Sorry," Coco whispered.

Power, who had glanced jovially at her, moved his eyes back to Karen's. "Anyway," he went on, "after the Seattle police took the good reverend's deposition—"

"Crossinggard came to them, did he?" Blixen asked. "Out of the blue? Yelling 'Chaplin was a Commie, Chaplin was a Commie'?"

"No, sir," Power said, "he did not. Seattle detectives tracked Crossinggard down. I'd asked them to check out some political information I'd received. About a letter Chaplin had written, containing certain threats—"

Karen's knees buckled. Blixen snaked an arm around her shoulders, but she recovered almost at once and elbowed him away.

Nevertheless Power had turned solicitous. "Ma'am, are you faint? Maybe we ought to—"

"You bugger off, Adolf! Just bugger off!"

Power smiled. "That's it, take a deep breath, ma'am," he said softly. "That's the stuff."

"I only want to know one thing—"

Butting in, Lucille said: "No, she doesn't! Nils, tell her to keep her trap shut—"

"What I want to know, mein Führer, is exactly who sold you this stinking information? Was it John MacVicar? Because when I talked to John not—"

"You *talked* to him?" Power barked. "When? Today?"

The ferocity of his attack silenced her.

"Miss Chaplin, Miss, Miss!" Power said and tugged at her in his enthusiastic astonishment and dropped her arm like a hot potato when she winced. "Sorry! Did I hurt you? I'm awfully sorry. Listen. When did you have this conversation with Dr. MacVicar?"

"I—called him from the shop—"

"And you argued? When he told you he was going to testify—"

"By God, I hear this, but I don't believe it!" Blixen exploded. "Power, either you're the world's biggest ass, or you *have* lost your mind! Look around you! You've got three, four, *five* civilian witnesses to your illegal browbeating—"

Hoarsely Power said: "Mr. Blixen—!" and pointed a rigid finger at him, but then swept his eyes around the circle of faces and lowered his arm. "Hell," he said. "Swinnerton—what's her last comment there?"

" 'I called him from the shop.' "

Power brooded for a couple of dark beats, then pivoted toward the door. "It'll have to do. Bring her along—"

"Just the suspect or the whole crowd?" Burkhardt asked.

"Just the suspect," replied Power. "Take the rest of their statements here and we'll—"

"Okay, I have *had* it, who's the police commissioner now?" Lucille rasped. "Jordan? Is it Charles Jordan? Does anybody know Charles Jordan? Clement, phone Jordan. Never mind. I'll do it." She tramped away, changed her mind, circled back to stand jaw to jaw and eye to eye with Power. "Because, buster, if you think you and your stooges have a mandate from heaven to ruin my party, delay my dinner, just so—"

"By the way, Mrs. Gompers," Power asked, "when did Miss Chaplin arrive here?"

Lucille drew her head back somewhat, focusing. "Arrive? Well, God, I don't remember—"

Blixen said: "It was about six-thirty, Sergeant."

Power regarded him lazily. "You picked her up?"

"Yes."

"At what time?"

"I can't be sure."

"Rough stab. Six o'clock? Four? Two?"

"Around six."

"For pity's sake, what does it matter?" Lucille fretted. "Is she expected to account for every second of every—"

"Why, no, ma'am, not every one," Power said and directed an avuncular twinkle at Karen. "Just the seventy-two hundred or so between one-thirty and three-thirty this afternoon. Once we have that little matter cleared up—"

"Then let's clear it up," Karen said. "I was in my shop. I was alone."

"Honey!" Lucille wailed.

Infuriated, Karen cried: "Oh, Lucille, cool it! It's none of your business! I don't want your help and I don't need your advice!" She wheeled again to Power. "I left about four! I got home at four-thirty!"

"When did you talk to Dr. MacVicar?"

"I have no idea! About one."

"Fought with him?"

"You bet I fought with him!"

"Slammed the phone down," Power said, "jumped in your car, drove over there—"

"Drove—what? No—"

"Oh, Christ," Blixen said and closed his eyes. In the darkness everything glittered; the pound of blood in his ears deafened him. But not enough to drown out Power's thready voice.

"Mists beginning to lift a little, Mr. B., are they?"

His own voice sounded as thin as a robot's. "He can't be dead. . . ."

"Yes, sir. Yes, he is, stone-dead."

"Who is?" Coco asked in the distance, and Gompers said: "John?" and went on repeating it, varying it: "Johnny? John? Who are they talking about, Johnny?" but for Blixen, and evidently for Power as well, there were only the two of them in the room, conversing in a funeral-paced echoing hush. "How?" Blixen whispered.

"Butcher knife in the stomach. Closing of the circle."

"How did you—"

"I needed a point cleared up. I called on him at ten minutes to five. I found him in the kitchen. He'd been dead for at least an hour and a half. He'd put up a fight. There was enough skin under his fingernails to upholster a davenport."

Out of the corner of his eye Blixen saw Karen's left hand fall from her other forearm.

Power had seen it, too. "So somebody," he went on softly, "has got a scratch on him the size of the Grand Canyon. Hasn't he."

He beckoned to Swinnerton. " 'Kay, kids," he said, "let's go."

II

The fragrant October evening was as fresh and warm and clear as the lovely day had been, though they all might have been milling about in the Arctic from the looks of them. Shaken and chilled they had followed Karen and the police out of the house one by one, but they seemed reluctant—except for Blixen—to go on to the curb. They didn't know how to address the problem, what to attack, whom to blame. Two of the three women wept; Mrs. De-Forrest repeated again and again that she wasn't surprised, that she was even relieved to hear the other shoe drop. But no one listened.

After Karen had crawled into the back of Power's gray Granada, Blixen stuck his head through the rear window to inform her that he'd follow the police downtown and would stay with her at least until Duffield arrived.

Showing him a face as casual and disengaged as a *Vogue* model's, Karen said: "But, darling, what on earth for?"

"I don't want you to be alone."

The bright, blank eyes rounded. "Oh, sweetheart, that's a dear offer, but it's not practical and it's not necessary. What can they do to me? Except smear ink on my fingertips and snap a couple of unflattering pictures? Besides, I'm used to being on my own." A faint smile touched her mouth. "I prefer it."

"I'll come anyway."

Behind him Power said: "Splendid! Means I can kill two birds with one stone." He beamed at Karen. "See, it'll give us a chance to record Mr. B.'s official statement. All about how the two of you spent the entire night of the graduation party together."

Karen leaned her head against the back of the seat and studied the roof light.

Power winked at Blixen, and started around to the driver's door.

"Sergeant," Blixen murmured.

Guileless as a baby, Power paused by the rear fender.

Blixen examined the curbside weeds at his feet for a reflective second or two, then raised his head and smiled.

Power smiled back.

"I take it," Blixen said, smiling, "that you don't have a great deal of faith in Miss Chaplin's alibi."

"For which murder?"

"Either one."

"Not a great deal, no."

"Well," Blixen said, "if Miss Chaplin is lying about the Kanaris killing—if we weren't together that night—then I have no alibi either. Have I?"

"Follows," said Power, "as the night the day."

"Yet you haven't arrested me."

Power's smile broadened. He peeked through the Granada's rear window at the two bowed heads in the back seat—Karen's and Swinnerton's—then touched Blixen's elbow and drew him into an amiable walk along the gutter. "Mr. Blixen," Power said, "may I be frank? Your name was bandied about. I won't deny it." He thrust out his lower lip judiciously. "But in the end, you see, we just couldn't close our eyes to Miss Chaplin's terrific motive. Kanaris had tried to blackmail her, according to Dr. MacVicar. Perhaps you weren't aware of that—"

"She filled me in," Blixen said. "I told her not to worry. I promised I'd take care of the problem. So how can you be sure that I didn't take care of it by killing John? To keep him from testifying?"

"Mr. Blixen, that isn't a motive, that's a romantic gesture."

"You know," Blixen said, "your inconsistency is staggering. On the one hand, you doubt that I spent graduation night with Miss Chaplin, and on the other you clear me of MacVicar's murder without a second thought."

"I don't need a second thought. You're not a murderer."

"But I confirmed Karen's alibi. So at the very least, I must be a liar."

"You confirmed it before you had a chance to think." Power peeked at Blixen past his nose, then touched his elbow again and aimed him back toward the Granada. "But tell me this," he continued. "What's going to happen in court. When you're on the witness stand. Under oath." A lift of the eyebrow. "Eh? What then?"

"Well, we'll just have to wait and see, won't we," Blixen said.

"I'll lay odds on what *won't* happen," said Power. "I'll bet dollars to doughnuts that you won't lie."

"Speaking of court," Blixen said, "I've been under the impression all these years that guilt had to be established beyond a reasonable doubt before a jury could convict."

"Essentially true."

"Which must mean—essentially—that no one except the accused could possibly have committed the crime."

"Yes. . . . What are you getting at?"

"I want to offer you," Blixen said, "a reasonable doubt. Another candidate. For the Kanaris killing. Gilbert DeForrest."

"*That's* your candidate?"

"He had a far better opportunity than Karen had. He had as explosive a motive. . . . Did you know about his motive?"

"It's your theory, Mr. B., you lay it out."

"Kanaris had sold Coco some pot. DeForrest found it. He swore he'd kill Kanaris if the man ever set foot on his property again. Despite the threat, Sophocles came back to the house at five minutes to one. He'd arranged to meet Karen in the gazebo at one o'clock for some kanoodling. But now he sees that the house is empty. At least he assumes it's empty. So he thinks: *Okay, why not move the assignation indoors?* He undresses upstairs. He heads for the backyard to meet his date. And in the kitchen he comes face to face with DeForrest. There's a knife on the drainboard. DeForrest grabs it, catches Sophocles on the driveway outside, and stabs him in the belly."

Power gave a soft, amused snort and plucked at his nose hairs.

"Strikes you as funny, does it?" Blixen asked.

"Not as funny as it'd strike a jury."

"Uh-huh," Blixen continued, "but suppose Duffield could produce a witness who had seen DeForrest burying the body that night."

They had resumed their snail's pace back toward the Granada. Now Power halted.

"Talking supposition, of course," Blixen said.

Power said: "I see." He continued on to his car, lifted one foot to the rear bumper, and brushed absently at some mud on his cuff. "Okay, in that case I'd say that this supposed witness was either lying or mistaken. Or that DeForrest had become an accessory after the fact by trying to clean up someone else's dirty work."

"Are you saying that you could accept DeForrest as an accomplice, but not as a murderer?"

"Oh, I think DeForrest could have committed murder," Power answered. He lowered his foot, found a handkerchief, wiped his fingers musingly. "DeForrest was a violent man, no question about it. Half the neighborhood was afraid of him. He slapped his wife around regularly. . . . Yes, he could have beaten Kanaris to death, shot him, strangled him. . . ." Power folded the handkerchief, cast Blixen a curious look. "But Kanaris was stabbed."

"Well?" Blixen said.

After a moment Power said: "Sir, who told you about the pot and the fight and the threats? Coco?"

"Coco's mother."

"And did she go on then to accuse her husband of the crime?"

"On the contrary. She said I'd laugh if I realized how funny the idea was."

"But she wouldn't fill you in on the joke—?"

"*Is* there a joke?"

Power pooched out his lips. "Well," he said. "Joke. Twist may be a better word. Let's call it a twist. You know about twists, Mr. B. Or you ought to, in your business. Here's a sweet one. Gilbert DeForrest's father was a butcher. Gil was terrified of the old man. Developed a phobia. Went to a psychologist. Psychologist says: 'Sonny, you're afraid of castration. Poof. Phobia's gone.' But it didn't go. It never went. Until the day he died, Gil DeForrest couldn't so much as touch a knife. Wouldn't undergo a cancer operation that might have saved him. Wouldn't even cut his own meat." Power's lips parted in the sweetest smile. "Mr. B.?" he said. "How could that man have *stabbed* anyone?"

With a farewell tug on his cap's bill, Power piled into the Granada, kicked the engine over, and wheeled in a wide U-turn back toward Hawthorne Avenue.

The Granada's grill passed within a foot and a half of Blixen. And there wasn't a mark on it.

CHAPTER ELEVEN

Disaster in Fantasy-Land

I

Foam-fringed, lush as Ireland, Oahu slid drowsily past Blixen's window.

He drank in the sails and the surfers, Diamond Head, Waikiki, Pearl and the *Arizona* and the slow circling tour boats. After a million air miles, Blixen could still be dazed by three landings: San Francisco at night, Lisbon at dawn, Honolulu in the middle of the morning. A shepherd's-crook curl brought the DC-10 around and down toward a baked field; Blixen's nose stayed pressed to the glass until the plane had stopped rolling. . . .

Outside, the Hawaiian air lapped at him like water. He loosened his tie and straggled after his fellow passengers into a cooler terminal where half a dozen young tour guides piped unfamiliar Anglo-Saxon names and waved placards expectantly. One of the placards proclaimed HAIL TO THE JEFE in red script and was being brandished by a young woman who looked like Paul Muni in a muu-muu and who was in fact the superlative Chicana actress Isabel Chavez. Beside Isabel, Barney Lewis flapped a lei of waxy yellow blossoms at Blixen and hollered: "Nils! Welcome to Paradise!"

The lei smothered him, settling into place around his neck.

He gripped Barney's hand and kissed Isabel. "Hello, sweetheart—"

Laughing, Isabel cried: *"Bienvenido, patrón!"* and added: "Jesus, you look like hell."

"Thanks—"

"Well, I always figure if you can't say something nice, don't say anything at all, but I couldn't just stand here with my mouth shut, could I? Slip your jacket off. You're white as a sheet."

"What did they do," Barney asked, "show you an old Irwin Allen movie?"

"I couldn't tell you," Blixen answered. "I didn't watch the movie. I drank and I thought."

"About what?"

"Old ghosts. Half-remembered dreams. Anyway, moving right along, how are things with you guys?"

"David's here," said Isabel.

Blixen twitched in surprise. "David? Sanderson?"

"Flew in last night." Isabel nodded. "Roland wanted a couple of scenes rewritten, so he sent out a call for the story editor, which the next thing we know here comes David, portable and all. He didn't even wave at me. Just took a room and went to work. I says, 'David, I'm your mistress, don't I at least rate a peck on the cheek?' The SOB never even looked up."

Blixen said: "Well—Barney—did Roland discuss these script changes with you?"

"Discuss." Barney frowned. "Actually I wouldn't say discuss so much as bludgeon."

"Ah, Barn, quit crabbing," said Isabel. "They work, don't they?"

"But," asked Barney, "are they necessary? That's the question."

"Wrong, Philistine. Is ballet necessary? Is *baseball?* What Roland's giving you is Art, for God's sake."

Smiling, Blixen said: "I take it you're a disciple."

"*Patrón,* when this man blocked his first scene, I thought I'd died and gone to heaven. He's daring, he's practical, he's supportive, he *communicates. Dios,* what a director. I'm in love, *patrón.*" Isabel eyed Blixen shrewdly. "And so are you, I think. I think that's what makes you stand up to the Philistines. You're in love with Roland's talent. *Verdad?*"

"*Quizás.*"

"Sure, it sticks out a mile. Murf sees it, too. That's why he believes he's already lost this battle he imagines he's in with Roland. I said to him, I said: 'Murphy, the man isn't your destroyer, he's

your leavening!' I said: 'Murphy, Roland and Nils want to help
you grow!'" Tired, she shrugged her shoulders. "But he can't see
it."

"Where is he, by the way?"

Barney said: "Back at the pool. He wanted to come, but he was
afraid his fans would mob him."

"Speaking of stars," Isabel said.

II

The "Stagg" company had rented one of the rooms behind the
Kahala lagoon for its location headquarters, so after Blixen had
tried, and failed, to track Murf down at the pool, Barney led the
way across the lagoon bridge into the Lanai wing where Roland,
he said, might still be working on the production board. "They've
got a stocked refrigerator in there," Barney told Blixen. "You can
fix yourself a drink, freshen up, unwind. If Roland's out, maybe
you could even take a little nap—"

It was a tempting notion. Ever since he'd parted from Karen at
Portland's Central Precinct, Blixen's heart had had a leaden bump
to it. Depression nagged at him. He had drowsed during the flight,
but had awakened as stiff and cheerless as a sinner on Judgment
Day. He began to pray that Roland was out.

"Here we are," Barney said. He stepped into an alcove near the
end of the corridor and rapped on the door.

"Come," Roland sang.

"Shoot, he's there," Barney said. "Okay, I'll go corral Carl, and
Murf if I can find him—and who else did you want at this
meeting?"

"Barn, let me get organized first," Blixen said. "I'll go over
things with Rolly and then contact you, how's that?"

"You won't need me in on these preliminaries?"

"No."

"Thank God."

"Where'll you be?"

"Pool!" Barney called and bustled off down the hall.

At the same time the alcove door was flung open. Roland
Phipps scowled at Blixen from under the brim of his baseball cap,
saw who it was, and threw up his arms, laughing and pink.

"Bubby!" he cried. He embraced Blixen, gave him a resounding kiss on the cheek, pulling him into the room. "Well, come on in! How the hell are you? Somebody said you were coming! Who was it? Maybe Barney. I've been up to my navel in work. I don't listen—"

The room was green and airy, Polynesian; doors opened onto a small lanai, where Roland had set up his curved, three-sectioned production board on a glass-topped table. He had relinquished his jodhpurs for tennis shorts, but the Hawaiian shirt and the baseball cap remained inviolate. He scrubbed his hands together. "Are you hungry? Can I order you a sandwich? Drink? There's scotch, rum, vodka, gin—"

"The only thing I covet at this point, Rolly, is a bathroom."

"Now that you'll have to handle on your own. Through the louvered doors by the bed there."

While Blixen relieved himself, Roland lolled in the doorway and lit a cigar and grinned through his clenched teeth. "So, Nils," he said, "how long can you stay?"

"Oh, I'm like the rabbit, Roland, wham-bam-thank-you-ma'am. I'll have to be back in Portland by tomorrow."

"Glorioski. You mean you'd fly all this way just to spend a couple of hours with us? It must be love."

"It must be."

"Good. Because for a minute there I wondered if it could have been panic."

Flushing the toilet, Blixen moved to the washbasin, and regarded Roland in the cabinet mirror.

"Panic," Roland repeated. "You know what panic is. That's when a producer's faggot star stamps his foot and says he'll just spit if he has to work with his awful director one more day."

Blixen wet a washcloth and pressed it against his eyes. "I don't suppose you'd have any aspirin."

"Bottom shelf."

Blixen found the bottle, shook out three tablets, and closed the cabinet door. This time the mirror surprised an expression of intolerable fatigue on Roland's face. He spotted Blixen watching him and stood erect, puffing on the cigar, grinning again.

"Well, the hell with it. *Ars gratia artis* and bugger the faggots. By the way, you know who your real star is, I hope."

"Of course. Isabel."

"Mercy, what a talent. The energy. The *grasp*. Wait'll this picture comes out. We'll all win Ernies."

"Emmies."

"Emmies, Ernies, Shernies. The point is you're a fool not to take better advantage of that child. You won't have her long."

"I know."

"If you know, why was she so light in the script? Don't you read this junk?"

"She isn't light."

"Not now she isn't," Roland said and struck another match and relit his cigar.

Blixen swallowed his aspirin, put his glass down, and slowly turned.

"I called your writer in," Roland said. "I wanted to consult with you. Really. But there wasn't time." He waved the match back and forth. "We added a couple of things," he said.

"*Did* you."

"Bubby," Roland said, "you're quivering, you're getting those budget blues again." He pushed himself away from the doorjamb. "Come on, I'll show you."

"Roland," Blixen began, but the director was already whistling his way through the main room toward the lanai, so after a moment Blixen dropped his lei into the washbasin and sighed and followed.

Outside, the air was oven-hot. Applause and shouts of surprise drifted across the lagoon; the Kahala dolphins, sleek as artillery shells, had gone into their afternoon act. Backwash from their efforts lapped at the shores of the lanai cove.

Fiddling with the production board on the glass-topped table, Roland said: "Here. Look at this. Pull up a chair." He unbuttoned his shirt to scratch at a bug bite. "Actually, there's good news and there's bad news. What do you want first?"

Absently Blixen said: "Take your pick." He walked to the edge of the cove, stood listening to the smack of the diving dolphins and the scattered bursts of audience applause. "Just don't tell me you're going to add more days."

"I'm going to add more days," Roland said. "That's the bad news."

"I thought it might be."

At Blixen's feet the waters shifted. A scarred dolphin angled onto its side and smirked up at him. Blixen squatted. "Well, where the dickens did you come from? And what are you doing way over here? Aren't you supposed to be in the show?"

"That's the tank's one girl," Roland explained. "The males are after her night and day, night and day, so she hides here during the performance. She figures they'll never find her, but they always do. She won't face the truth."

"What truth?"

"That you can't hide from a screwing."

In the main lagoon, the male dolphins raced and postured. The scarred girl showed Blixen a flirtatious dorsal fin and sank into the safe depths.

"Don't you want to hear the good news?" Roland asked.

"Give me the good news," Blixen murmured.

"Very well, the *good* news," Roland said, "is that I discovered a foolproof way to save your ass. I've taken this mundane crap you call a story and given it grandeur. Now pay attention, because I don't want to have to go over this again and again." Roland raised a finger. "I've deemphasized," he said, "the police investigation."

Presently Blixen picked a blade of grass to chew on. "Roland," he said, "without the police investi—"

"I didn't say I eliminated it, I said I deemphasized it. I made an analysis of the script's structure, and I found that every single dramatic turning point, every crucial confrontation, occurred offscreen. From the murder to—"

"We're doing a mystery, Roland. If you see the murderer there's no mystery."

"Tell that to Columbo."

"I'm not producing 'Columbo,' I'm producing 'Stagg at Bay.' "

"You're producing crap, Nils!"

"But it's crap you agreed to contribute to when you okayed the script."

"I okayed the basic *story!*" Roland cried. "I don't do *scripts,* I make *pictures! My* pictures, out of *my* guts, *my* talent! Scripts are for toilet paper! Who pays any attention to scripts?"

"I do," Blixen said.

"Nils—!" Roland burst out, and then swept off his baseball cap and rubbed the sweat from his bald head. He brooded for a few seconds. "Okay, look," he said. "I'm a reasonable man. I understand your point of view. You're the producer and you worry about money. Good. I'll make you a trade. Cut my throat and hope to die, I'll do my very best to regain my lost time and to keep your budget overage to a minimum. And all you'll have to give me in return is a little artistic freedom."

After a moment, Blixen said: "To do what?"

"Deemphasize the police investigation, show the murder, tell the story through Isabel's eyes, cut your faggot star down to his key scenes, and win you an Ernie. Emmy."

Blixen rose, spat out the grass blade, and returned his gaze to the lagoon.

"You're happier already," Roland said. "I can tell. You *look* happier."

"I just realized my headache's gone."

"Of course it's gone. They don't call me old Doc Phipps for nothing. So it's a deal?"

"No, sir," Blixen said, "no deal."

Roland, who had started back toward the glass-topped table, stopped short. Presently he turned. "You don't trust me, do you? You don't believe I can make up that lost time."

"I know you can't," Blixen said.

"Nils, when I tell you—"

"Because you're off the picture, Roland."

Overhead, a burst of wind from the sea clattered through the palm fronds.

Roland's pale blue eyes never moved, never shifted from Blixen's.

There was a cane-backed chair near Blixen's hand. He lifted it, reversed it. "Sit down," he said quietly. "Let's talk." He waited for a response, shrugged when none came, and moved toward the sliding glass door.

"Freeze," Roland said. He picked up the cigar he'd deposited in a crystal ashtray beside the production board. He studied the gray ash. "Nils," he said, and cleared his throat, "you know, if this is a TV-type joke, I'm not laughing."

"It's no joke."

"*You* are firing *me? Why?*"

"Because you're not the man for the job."

The old voice grew feather-soft. "But you hired me. Why was that?"

Blixen turned it over in his mind. His forearms had begun to ache. He forced his fists open, splayed the fingers. "Maybe," he said and paused, and then continued: "I think it must have been because I couldn't see the truth past all the respect I had for you. Isabel told me I was in love with your talent. She was right. You're the finest director in the business, in my opinion."

"So how do you reward the finest director in the business? You give him the boot." Spewing laughter and smoke, half-strangled, Roland barked: "Mother of heaven, what a story! I can see the *Variety* headline now. 'TV Sausage-Maker Cans Academy Laureate.'" He sucked hungrily at the cigar. "Not the man for the job how."

"Roland, there's no point in—"

"Say, you were the one who wanted to talk!" Roland screamed. "All right, you talk! Talk!"

Blixen regarded his white knuckles for a silent second. "Roland," he said, "I produce miniatures. You're a muralist. I can't fit you onto my canvas. I can't contain your splash. What I need is a director who understands diplomacy and cooperation, discipline, budget—"

Eyes bulging, Roland cried: "Well, how do you think I *began?* I shot a feature a month for Yates at Republic! I *lived* on Poverty Row! I thought you liked spice in your sausage! Okay, I was wrong! I'll take it out. . . . What are you shaking your head for?"

"Because it won't work."

"No?" Incredulously Roland looked around the cove for support. "I don't believe this. I'm begging the man to let me play in his manure pile. Because that's what he produces, manure. He's produced so much manure that he can't smell perfume when it's smeared under his nose." In a sudden rage, Roland slammed his cigar to the ground and bent, shouting, toward Blixen. "Why, you pitiful pinhead, I gave you a pan that *Eisenstein* couldn't have filmed, and you've got the *gall* to—!"

Blixen said: "I'll contact your agent tomorrow. We'll honor the full commitment."

"You come back here! Come back here!"

Blixen stepped into the guest room, retrieved his jacket and tie from the bed where he'd dropped them, and continued toward the hall door.

"Nils, you're killing me!" Roland shouted. "You know how this bloody business works! I haven't made a picture in three years! They'll say I can't hack it anymore! Don't throw me to the wolves, Nils!"

Blixen halted halfway into the alcove, head down, eyes shut.

Encouraged, Roland trotted after him. "Bubby, it's dumb to fight like this! We need each other. Forget artistic freedom. I'll shoot your silly script—"

Outside, the dolphin show was over; the admiring audience had drifted away. From the shaded end of the cove came a half-human shriek. The water churned and frothed.

The males had found their scarred girl again.

"Okay, bubby?"

Without a word Blixen closed the guest-room door behind him and walked out of the alcove and down the corridor.

III

Neither Murf nor Barney had returned to the pool.

After circling the tanning area twice, Blixen made his way to the front desk, coaxed the number of David Sanderson's room out of the young lady there, and took the elevator to the ninth floor.

Before he'd rounded the corner at the end of the elevator bank, he heard the crabbed tap of the typewriter.

Someone had wedged Sanderson's door open; in the room's entranceway, Isabel stood with her back to Blixen, flapping a towel vigorously.

"Is that aerobics," Blixen muttered into her ear, "or are you surrendering?"

Isabel shrieked and spun, one hand to her chest. "Christ, you scared me to *death!*" she exclaimed. "Where did you *come* from!"

"Elevator. I'm sorry. Soft carpets—"

"Well, *cough* next time! Is my hair pure white? Jesus. Some choice. Either I suffocate in there with the demon pipe-smoker, or I crawl out here and you scare me blind."

"So the towel—?"

"I thought I'd try to churn up a little draft—"

"Open a window."

"They *are* open! All of them!" Isabel drew her eyebrows together. "*Patrón,* are you anemic? You look worse than you did when you landed. I swear you're the only man I ever heard of who could come to Hawaii and get paler—"

In David's room the typing rattled to a clamorous stop. "Goddamn it," Sanderson shouted hoarsely, "will you two blabbermouths either shut up or go swimming or something! Hi, Nils!"

"Hi, David."

"I'll dig you later, okay? I've got one more act to finish! Close the door when you leave! *Mahalo!*"

Ignoring him, Isabel murmured: "Really, I've never seen you this strung out. Did you run into Murf? Did you have a fight?"

"Not with Murf," Blixen said. He smiled a little at the perplexity in Isabel's eyes and patted her cheek. "Come inside," he said. "I want to talk to you and the demon smoker."

Isabel stared at the towel in her hands, folded it, and moved past Blixen into the room.

"AAAARGH!" Sanderson shouted. "I ASKED you—!"

"Ah, stuff a plug in it," Isabel growled. "And comb your hair. Here's the producer."

Wild-eyed, Sanderson staggered up from the low corner sofa when Blixen entered. A portable typewriter was positioned on the coffee table in front of him; paper in stacks and shreds and crumpled balls littered the floor. He had removed his shirt, but despite the sweat-tangled hair on his chest and the ink smudges across his jaw and the corncob pipe in his mouth, he still contrived to appear thin-nosed and patrician. Blue rum-flavored smoke hung in shifting layers from the ceiling. Slapping at it, Sanderson wheezed: "Nils, you catch me at the worst possible time. Naturally Roland wants to shoot the big action tomorrow morning and I haven't even started to think it through yet, so if you could just—"

"David, fear not," Blixen said, "for, behold, I bring you good tidings of great joy. You're off the hook. You can cover your typewriter. We're going back to the original script."

Behind him the bed creaked as Isabel plunked onto it.

Sanderson felt for the low sofa with his calves and sat down, too.

"Don't everybody talk at once," Blixen said.

"Original script," Sanderson said.

Blixen nodded.

"Huh," Sanderson said. He gave the stack of papers on the coffee table a vague tap, stuck his pipe in his mouth again, and puffed.

Blixen said: "Naturally I wish you could have been spared all the extra work—"

"Hey. Ours not to reason why." Sanderson displayed a ghastly grin around the pipe stem. "Matter of fact I wondered where the money for this budget-buster was supposed to come from. It's just—" His eyes slid toward the bed. "Well, I mean, Isabel had some scenes she could sink her teeth into. . . ."

"I realize that. I'm sorry."

"Sorry," Isabel repeated in a croaky, dangerous undertone. "There's a comforting word. Who sabotaged us? Arthur Todd or the network?"

After a moment Blixen turned. "Neither one. It was my decision."

"Sure, defend the bastards." She sat hunched forward on the end of the bed, forearms crossed over her stomach. *"Dios,* when Roland hears . . . Well, it's academic." She lifted her head. "Because this man doesn't know how to compromise! He'll tear the bloody network up and have it for breakfast! And shoot the film the way he wants. What do you do then?"

"Then I remove him."

Her eyes jeered. "Come on—"

"Hijita," Blixen murmured, "it's already been done. He's off the picture."

There was a sharp crack as Sanderson bit through his pipe stem.

Isabel uncrossed her arms. She sat back, hands flat on the bed flanking her ample hips. "Removed him," she said. Disbelieving, she heaved herself to her feet. "You," she said, "removed a man who has more talent in the hangnail of his little finger than all the stumblebums you foisted on us have got in their combined bloated bodies? You removed Roland *Phipps?*"

"Isabel," Sanderson muttered.

Blixen said: "It's all right, David."

"It's *not* all right!" Isabel shouted. "All right, bull! Do you know what Roland's plans were? They went to the heart of that rotten story! They *illuminated* it! They—they—they pushed your mumble-mouthed star offscreen long enough to let the rest of us *act*—to let us *develop* and breathe and *live,* and you—" She had begun to choke on her own fury. Tears streamed down her brown cheeks. "And don't think I'm crying either, because I'm not! The man," she shouted, crying, "hasn't been born who could make me cry, and don't you forget it!"

"Here," Sanderson said, but she slashed his hand and his handkerchief aside and instead went galloping out onto the narrow balcony that overlooked the lagoon, and buried her face in her hands and wept her heart out.

At last Sanderson cleared his throat, balled up his handkerchief and stuffed it into his hip pocket. "So, Nils," he said, "how was the trip? How was Portland?"

"Oh, about as dramatic as Honolulu," Blixen said.

From the entryway, someone mumbled: "Anybody home? It's me, Barn."

"Yeah, Barn," Blixen answered. "Come on in."

With an expression of paralyzing disingenuousness on his face, Barney Lewis put his head around the entryway corner. "The door was open," he explained, "but I couldn't tell if anybody—"

"Never mind, come in, come in," Blixen said. "Got something to check out with you."

"Yeah, okay," Barney said.

"Barn," Blixen asked, "do you still carry a DGA card?"

On the balcony Isabel snuffled and Barney, who had just then succeeded in dragging his fascinated gaze away from her, gave up and let his head swing back again. "A—well, sure, Nils, I'm current," he said vaguely. "I mean you never know when some—"

"How'd you like to direct the two-parter?"

Lurching, Sanderson struck his shin on the coffee table and fell onto the sofa, cursing and red-faced and clutching his leg above his wound.

"I believe," Blixen said, "that Mr. Sanderson may have a comment here."

"Comments," Sanderson hissed. "My leg's shattered in eighteen places and you talk comments. Screw comments. You're the producer."

"That's true," Blixen said. He looked at Barney. "Well?"

By now Barney had ratcheted his head around. He wet his lips with the tip of his tongue. "I wonder," he said, "if something could have slipped by me back there—"

"I asked you if you'd care to direct the two-parter."

Back and forth flicked Barney's eyes, concentrating first on one Blixen pupil, then the other. "Roland's sick?"

"Roland's out."

"I'll fill you in later," Sanderson grunted.

Barney flicked his gaze to Sanderson and returned it to Blixen. "Yeah," he whispered. "Okay."

"Can you do it? No doubts? No vapors?"

"Nothing," Barney said. "I'll even bring it in on budget. Sort of."

"David, tell me," Blixen said, "how many of Isabel's new scenes can be incorporated into the old script without wrecking the basic structure?"

Sanderson flung a swift look at the figure on the balcony. He started to rub the bowl of the pipe on his nose but desisted, wincing, when the cob scratched him. Slowly he said: "Well—two at least. Her two best ones."

"Do you know the scenes he's talking about, Barney?"

Sanderson said: "The thing on the bridge, Barn, and the revelation after the car wreck."

"Okay, right," Barney said. "I approve."

"That's it, then," Blixen said. He consulted his watch. "I'm due at the airport. I won't have time to see Murf. Give him my love, will you?"

"I'll kiss him full on the lips," Barney said. "But don't you want to stay until—"

"I can't. If you run into trouble, call me. . . . Goodbye, David —*hijita*—"

Without turning, Isabel said: "You take one more step toward that door, *hombre*, and I'll put out a contract on you."

Blixen stopped by the bed.

"Everybody else beat it," Isabel grated. "Go on, hurry up."

"Ah, David," Barney said brightly, "why don't me and you go downstairs and have a beer and ogle the chicks and chat about your changes. More or less in that order. What do you say?"

Sanderson's face was still worried, but when Blixen smiled at him, he sighed and said: "Yeah, why don't we," and pushed himself off the sofa and limped after Barney into the entranceway. There he paused to look back one more time at Isabel before shrugging and leaving and letting the door slam.

"Dear David and his doubts and his big sighs," Isabel said wearily. "He's afraid I'm going to light into you again. How can somebody I love so much know so little about me?"

"It's a puzzle."

Isabel dug her thumbs hard into her eye-sockets and at last turned to face Blixen. "But you understand me, don't you? When I rant and rave and holler, David sees a crazy-mad woman. What do you see?"

"A scared one."

Isabel made a scornful noise deep in her larynx, a sort of a jaded snicker, but almost before it was out, her mouth had begun to crumple and soon she was marching blindly toward him, wailing. "Oh, *patrón*, why don't you smack me when I dump on you like that! I am such a *slob!*"

Murmurous, full of laughter and reassurance, Blixen hugged her close, rocking her, remembering another tearful scene, another weeping woman. . . .

"Oh, don't deny it!" Isabel cried dramatically. "There's a word for me in Old English! Clinchpoop!"

"Clinchpoop?"

"I am a *clinchpoop!* A clod and a boor and a—"

"You're not a clinchpoop."

"And do you know what the height of clinchpoopery is? It's when you realize the other guy's right but you won't say so because you're too bloody selfish!" She reared back to glare at Blixen out of swollen red eyes. "Because the righter I admitted you were to myself, the more I hated you for taking my big new scenes away! Who needs truth when selfishness is so satisfying? I'm not as dumb as I look, believe me. The minute Roland outlined his new concept, I recognized it was wrong—I felt it was unbalanced—it was like, oh, like redoing *Gone With the Wind* and throwing all the best lines to Aunt Pittypat. It's Stagg's show, it's *got* to be Stagg's show! But when you asked me to face that, I just—" Isabel jammed her head against Blixen's chest, sank her fingernails into his forearms. "God, *patrón,* how did *you* face it? You picked him. You were in love with his talent. How do you see truth past *love?*"

She lay lax and trembling against him, heavy in his arms, lover-heavy. Outside, two pigeons stretched and strutted. Searching for beheaded peanuts?

"*Patrón?* How?"

"Dimly. Sometimes never."

"No," Isabel countered, "I don't agree. I think if you're strong enough, and you ache for something bad enough, even truth, you'll find it. I think it's the self-kidders, like me, who fall flat on their faces. The mind just goes blank. Goes up. Like an actor who can't remember a single line."

"And what," whispered Blixen, "does the actor do then?"

"Well," Isabel said, pondering, "if she's me, she puts a dreamy look on her face and shuts up and listens to God."

Blixen's lips stirred on her forehead.

"You're laughing at me," Isabel said. "Don't you believe in God?"

"I can't, *hijita.*"

"Then what *do* you believe in?"

"Love. Life—"

"Truth?"

"Truth, yes."

"*Patrón,* you've just defined God."

Watching the pigeons, Blixen rubbed his chin gently across the top of her head. "And—this works? The lines come back? Because of your dreamy look?"

"Oh, not because of the look. The look is for mood. No, it's the shutting up that works. Plus the listening." Isabel drew back again to study his face. "But you have to ache for it, *patrón.* I guess that's where the strength comes in."

The pigeons flew away.

"Yes," Blixen said. "I guess it must be. . . ."

CHAPTER TWELVE

Listening

I

When Leo Tolstoy was young, he was invited to join a secret club his brother had organized. He succeeded in passing every initiation test save one. He never was able to stand in a corner for five minutes and not think of a white bear.

Nevertheless, Blixen thought, *try again.*

Draw the shade on the enormous Pacific night; there's nothing to be seen at this height anyway. Dinner's over. Headset's off. Movie's on. Eyes are closed.

Listen.

II

Airplane drone.

Coughs. Laughter.

His legs ache.

The laughter increases; the movie, for a wonder, may be worthwhile.

No.

Listen:

"Conjures up a curious picture, doesn't it? Now what do you suppose that ugly Greek gardener was doing out there in the buff?"

"Mick's dead."

"That bloody war! Just give me a second. It's the codeine. My whole head hurts. I was so surprised when I walked in. I still can't imagine what it means, can you?"

It means—

Rippling laughter.

"—buff—in the buff—"

"I had a chance to go into my dad's clothing store. Guess what I'm involved in now. Journalism. I bought a little West Side sheet. I'm the editor, Lucille handles circulation."

Yes, well, of course that's been the basic problem for the past hour, his circulation. To stop the ache in his legs, he really ought to slip out of his seat, stretch, find the lavatory. . . . He sneaks a look at the screen, where a raunchy blonde in jeans is trying to hitch a ride on a desert road. Blixen feels that this is the wrong approach entirely, that men would far rather rescue women in dresses and nylons. Ask Claudette Colbert. To whom it happened one night. Now—where is the lavatory? He hasn't had a chance to relieve himself since his stopover in Roland's room. In his mind's eye, he sees the three aspirins in his cupped palm; he closes the cabinet door, surprises the expression of intolerable fatigue on Roland's face—a closet light jiggles—

Codeine.

Aspirin.

"He must have sold his diamond stickpin and his jewelry box with the mirror on top because they weren't there either."

Listen!

He's talking to Power and Clem.

"Power, what did you just say?"

"Eh?"

"Something doesn't fit. You were talking about something, and I thought to myself: No, that's not true, that can't be true—"

"John W. Smith? Was it before that? The girl friend?"

Fruit closet. Blood. Blood everywhere. On the walls. On the clothing—head to toe—

There is a neck-snapping lurch; the plane falls—recovers—presses everyone's shoulders ear-high.

Screams. Nervous giggles. Someone across the aisle has gotten drenched with his own drink.

"Ladies and gentlemen, this is Captain Almayer? Hit a little air pocket there. Sorry about that. No harm done—"

Except that the thread of Blixen's thought has gone altogether. He had had the answer in his ears. He knows he had had it. And now he has nothing.

III

That morning the plane had taken off into a sky as cleansed and deep and pure as Crater Lake. It returned to a storm-doused city on a night as joyless as Blixen's own state of mind. The half-empty terminal smelled of wet overcoats; lovers fought; lost children wailed. To add to Blixen's gloom, he realized just as he stepped onto the parking lot tram that he had forgotten where he'd parked his rented Cadillac.

Rain cascaded down the tram windows. It proved impossible to see more than a foot or two into the thunderous night. But just as he had about decided to give up the chase, the familiar sunroof went gliding by and he jumped to his feet and shouted: "This one, driver!"

The tram groaned to a stop; the middle doors collapsed open. Blixen hesitated, staggered by the force of the rain, until the passenger behind him bumped into his back, and then he muttered: "Sorry," and vaulted onto the curb and into a glass-sided kiosk. His fellow passenger scrambled after him and the tram squished away.

Bloody night, Blixen thought. He started into the storm, but drew back when lightning split the sky.

"Whooooeee," said his companion. He was a pale teenager, unsuitably dressed and shaking with cold. He buried his hands in his blazer pockets, teeth chattering. Rain dripped off the bill of his cap.

"I hope you're parked closer to this thing than I am," said Blixen.

"Yeah, I ain't too far," the boy answered.

Lightning danced along the horizon; thunder reverberated.

Bloody night. Bloody rain. Bloody life. The thunder is like the clang of iron shovels against stone, the roll of dirt down a graveside. He hurries up the drive, and there they are—Sophocles in the ditch and, bent over him, covered with blood—

"With *blood?*" Blixen said aloud. And then, stupidly: "Blood? Blood?"

There is a sound that tumblers make when the proper key is pressed against them—a kind of a silken chunk—that is as orgasmic in its own way as a sneeze. The bolt has relaxed. The door is not yet open, but the lock has given up.

One need only twist the knob to see the prize. The face. The answer. The truth.

Breathlessly Blixen twisted toward the boy behind him, and the first bullet entered his side halfway between his right hip and his lowest rib, burned a two-inch furrow before plowing free, and shattered the glass wall of the kiosk.

It smashed him backward. The noise of it was deafening, although the gun in the boy's hand seemed as dainty as a comic cigarette lighter. He slipped down the wall onto his bottom, his legs spread-eagled and numb. *But there's no dignity at all to it,* he thought. Actors died with such panache and dishonesty. He put his hand against his ripped coat and examined the slow leak of his blood, which was a major mistake because the sight of the blood, the reality of the blood, seemed to unblock the shocked circuits in his brain, to let the pain flare up from the torn nerve endings.

Again the deafening boom. But this time a shaky aim sent the bullet skipping off the pavement into the ranks of cars. A horn blasted. Someone yelled.

It was too much for the boy. He dropped the gun and was already flapping toward the rain when Blixen caught at one dirty ankle and brought him crashing to the ground and drew him like milk up a straw back into the kiosk and reached for the grimy throat. *Blessed if that cab driver wasn't right,* Blixen thought, *a snot-nosed sixteen-year-old.* And aloud he said: "You've ruined my jacket," and gripped the throat and pounded the head again and again onto the kiosk floor, was still pounding it when the first shocked passerby clattered up to pull him away. . . .

IV

Flashes of light.

"Somebody's got his knee in my side," Blixen said.

He seemed to be in a darkened Quonset hut. Ribbed walls breathed beside his stretcher. The next time a whitish shape leaned over him, he said: "Do you know what the second worst cliché in TV is?"

"What's the first?"

" 'Let's get out of here.' "

"What's the second?"

"It's 'Where am I?' "

"Well, maybe they're clichés because people have this great need of them."

"I believe you're right. Where am I?"

"You're in the recovery room at Providence Hospital."

"Oh, I can't tell you how happy that makes me. I'm recovering then?"

"Yes, you're recovering."

"Let's get out of here," Blixen said.

V

He awoke depressed and thirsty. His first impression was that he was trapped at the bottom of the sea, perhaps imprisoned in a small glass aquarium. The air was green and undulant; rain beat against curtained windows. He ran the tip of his tongue over his dry lips and croaked: "Water," and someone held a tumbler containing a glass straw against his chin. He sipped, gazing at Power.

"Good morning," Power said.

When he had sipped his fill, he let the glass straw fall away from his mouth. "Conrad," he said, "this is a very violent town."

"No, it's not," Power said. "You just attract trouble."

"What time is it?"

"Ten-thirty Monday morning."

"Did you catch the kid?"

"We didn't have to catch him, we had to rescue him."

"He's the snot-nosed sixteen-year-old who tried to run me down Friday. You didn't hear about that."

"Yes, I heard. Miss Chaplin told me. She said you figured I'd done it."

"He was hired. He'd probably been following me all night—up to the house in the hills—over to Vista. He's got a gray Granada. I know who hired him."

Expectantly Power replaced the glass on the bedside table.

Blixen stared at the bars of his bed.

"So give me a name," Power said.

"I *knew* who hired him," Blixen said. "Don't interrupt me."

Power waited.

"I had it all laid out. . . . Chapter and verse. I saw every trick, every lie. . . ." Exhausted, Blixen exhaled. "I can't reach it."

"No sweat. The kid'll tell us. He's an addict. Twenty-four more hours and he'll be happy to betray his own mother." Power slapped his knees and stood. "Go to sleep. I'll see you tomorrow when your mind's clearer."

VI

All afternoon long, Blixen thinks and drowses and fashions his speculative web like a spider in a warm barn window. By supper-time he has reconstructed the conversation with Power, and has picked out the phrase that hadn't fit. Over the vanilla pudding, he ponders MacVicar's addled expression when they'd talked in front of the fire. Recalls MacVicar's querulous consternation. *"But I had so much to think about. I was so surprised when I walked in. I still can't imagine what it means, can you? Well, I'll check it out tomorrow. . . ."*

One question especially nags: Why had the body in the De-Forrest ditch been naked?

It does not help that a nurse bustles in to feed him a sleeping pill the moment his tray is whisked off. Nevertheless, in the semi-darkness of his private room, in the stillness of his relaxed mind, one startling conversation at the Gompers party does replay itself.

It is between Mrs. DeForrest and him.

It concerns the missing diamond stickpin.

Now he sees motive as well as killer.

His head whirls; the sleeping pill is doing its job. He'll contact the police in the morning.

But just as he is drifting off, why, naturally, bang, a second nurse pushes his door open.

Except that it isn't a nurse.

It's the killer.

CHAPTER THIRTEEN

You Commit Murder

Blixen turned his head on the hard damp pillow.

"Hi, Nils-Frederik," the killer said.

"Hi, Lucille," said Blixen.

The door sighed shut behind her. She remained fixed in the shadows, hands clasped over her purse below her little paunch. "My, what a neat room. . . . Darling, no, no! Don't call out, for heaven's sake. You'll rouse the whole hospital. Waken the poor sickies, eh?"

"Wouldn't like to do that," Blixen said.

"Well, no." She gave a tuba-deep belch, covered her mouth at once. But the flowery fragrance of good gin had slipped through. "I *do* beg your pardon," she said.

It was grotesque. The sense of menace was unmistakable, but unmistakably trembling at the same time on the edge of farce, like a Hitchcock resolution. Who but Hitch would slip his hero a potent sedative just when his reactions should be sharpest? Or present his threat with her slip showing?

"I am *exhausted,*" Lucille said. "Talk about your blue Mondays. Well, I'm sure it hasn't been any barrel of roses for you either. I never meant for him to hurt you, Nils. If I told that rotten boy once, I told him a dozen times, shoot straight—" She stopped. "Or am I spilling the beans here? You have a sort of a distrait look on your face. Don't you know what I'm talking about?"

"Yes, I know, Lucille."

"Well, that's a relief. I presumed you did but I couldn't be positive. I mean, you seemed so unpositive yourself. You kept saying you couldn't remember and all."

"I couldn't."

"But you finally did?"

"Most of it."

"Me standing over that driveway ditch with the shovel?"

"Yes."

"I was afraid you would. Eventually." She dragged up a chair, sank onto it, moody, pressured. Faintly insane? "And now you'll tell the cops, won't you?"

"Well—"

"Oh, you will, you will, you're the type. I never should have hired that tacky kid. That was the move of a complete ninny. If you want something done right, do it yourself."

"Where did you find him?"

"Downtown—on Salmon. The poor little chaps hang around the arcades and offer their bods for fixes and so on. So I promised him a hundred dollars if he'd bump you off. Well, he was ecstatic. He *assured* me he was an absolute expert, but I don't believe the little liar had so much as stepped on a bug before, do you?" Disheartened, Lucille pushed her long sleeves back, picked a fallen pillow off the floor. "Well—"

"Uh—Lucille—"

"Oh, now, Nils, grow up!" Lucille said fiercely. "Suffocation doesn't hurt, and it has to be done—"

Nothing worked but his instinct. The sedative lay like lead in his arms and legs. The pillow would cut off his first peep. There was a heavy pitcher of beaded water on a table not half a foot from his head and he couldn't lift a finger to reach it. Even his tongue had thickened. "Well, yes, but isn't that the point? *Does* it have to be done? What does killing me accomplish now that Power has the kid? He's an addict. He's bound to confess sooner or later that you hired him. And why."

"He has no idea why. I told him we were part of a love triangle, and I was acting out of passion."

"You didn't."

"What's so funny about it? I used to think the world of you, Nils. Maybe you came back and started sniffing around Karen and I flipped. Murder two at the most. Meanwhile, you won't be here to tell what you saw thirty years ago."

"But Power'll be able to untangle that by himself, Lucille. He's a very bright man."

"He's not a bit bright." Nevertheless, she sat down again, smoothed the pillow over her lap. "In any case, I have a valid alibi for the Alameda murder. Sophocles was alive and well when Clemmie and I went to Seaside. Clemmie'll swear I wasn't out of his sight for a minute." She cast a sidelong glance at Blixen. "How's Power going to get around that?"

"The same way I got around it. By figuring out who the real victim was."

Lucille's eyes remained steady on his.

"Power's a bulldog, Lucille. Which means he's too good a detective not to reopen the case when he sees me dead. He'll go back to the bones. He'll go back to Heitkemper. He'll subpoena the dental records if he has to."

Lucille's hands grew still on the pillow.

"And then," Blixen said, "he'll find that the X rays were switched. That the jaw under the driveway wasn't Sophocles'."

"And," Lucille murmured, "just whose jaw was it, pray?"

"It was Gil DeForrest's."

Smiling, contemptuous, Lucille looked away and shook her head.

"Because DeForrest," Blixen went on, "didn't die of cancer in Chicago, did he? He was stabbed to death—by you—sometime around eleven o'clock on the night of the party. By the time Clem picked you up, DeForrest was buried and you were back in the upstairs bedroom."

"Darling, Gilbert died in his wife's arms—of cancer—in Chicago! That's the fact."

"That's a lie. Somebody was buried—or cremated—under DeForrest's name. But I very much doubt that he died in Agnes's arms. I think he was in the morgue when she got there. I think he was an unclaimed vagrant. And I think Agnes claimed him and identified him and paid for his cheap funeral."

"*Why?*"

"For twenty-one hundred dollars."

"Oh, *Nils!*"

"She was broke, Lucille. She was scared. Her husband may have skipped the country—"

"He *wrote* to her twice!"

"No. She *claims* he wrote to her twice. But no one saw the letters. Not even Coco. At any rate—the man was gone, and all he'd left behind was a five-thousand-dollar insurance policy. And even that had been borrowed against. Still—twenty-one hundred dollars might let Agnes squeak through until Coco could begin earning bigger money. But there had to be a death certificate. So Agnes picked a town as far from Portland as a bus would carry her, and went looking for a likely corpse. No insurance company was about to fight over twenty-one hundred dollars—"

Lucille's fleshy nose had grown pinched and disdainful. "And you honestly expect Conrad Power to go along with this fairy tale? Nils, really—"

"No," Blixen said, "what I expect Power to do—sooner or later —is recheck the dental records."

Lucille grimaced wearily.

"Lucille," Blixen murmured, "come to your senses. You can't alter a fact by denying it. If Power digs deeply enough into Heitkemper's records, he'll find the truth. Can't you see that?"

At last Lucille sighed and shut her tired eyes. "Oh, God. All right. Yes, I suppose so."

The room had begun to tilt and swim; Blixen forced his nails into his palms. "Tell me—how did you convince Heitkemper to switch the X rays?"

"I didn't have to convince him. He suggested it. The minute the skeleton was dug up. He's in love with me."

Blixen stared at her.

"Oh, don't look so shocked," Lucille said. "It's been beautiful. It started the summer after graduation. He was fifty, the most exciting man I'd ever seen." Her cheeks reddened.

"But you married Clem."

"Girls had to marry *somebody* in those days, darling. And Dwayne was already married. And Clemmie was there—" She plucked at a snag in the pillowcase. "The problem was that I couldn't talk to Clement. We could fool around in back seats, go swimming, laugh. But not talk."

Blixen woke with a start, and stretched his eyes.

"See, after the murder," Lucille was saying, "I had to be held— or I would have exploded. Well, I'd known Dwayne all my life. I mean, he'd always fixed my teeth—"

"So you seduced him—confessed to the killing—"

"Yes."

"And that didn't turn Dwayne off?"

"It excited him," Lucille said. "He'd make me repeat the story over and over. I can't imagine why."

"Tell *me* the story."

She raised her eyebrows. "I thought you knew it."

"I do."

Lucille gave a brisk nod, settled herself in the chair, knees together, as defiant and receptive as a new pupil in a front-row seat. "You tell it then."

For a moment Blixen remained still, laboring to arrange his thoughts.

Restlessly Lucille crossed her legs, tugged her skirt down, laughed. "I warned you we'd end up in a Charlie Chan finish," she said. "Well, there's no Number One son, and you didn't invite the rest of the suspects in, but still—"

"Lucille, be serious. This is a very complex business."

"Oh, excuse me for living," Lucille said.

"Now," Blixen said. "We were in the rose garden. You'd gone outside to be sick, and I stumbled over you. You were lying just off the path. I even remember what you had on—a white party dress, nylons—"

"I'm impressed."

"I told you Clem was looking for you, and you went into the house to have a nap because you didn't want him to see you like that. Okay, you had your nap—and you woke up—oh, about ten-thirty, quarter of eleven. The party was over. Coco was gone, her mom, all the guests. You thought the house was empty. So you decided it was safe to cruise around a little."

Lucille watched him closely.

"You went back to the bedroom, opened a few drawers," Blixen said. "You found a jewelry box. There was a stickpin inside—"

"Yes, with four little diamonds in the center," Lucille said. "Exquisite. And then, too, it was quite small. I didn't think it would be missed. At least not for a while."

Blixen said: "You stole the jewelry box—you walked out of the bedroom—and you saw that the house wasn't empty after all. You ran into Gilbert DeForrest—"

"Wrong," Lucille said. "He ran into me. He came into the bedroom. Absolutely starkers, not a stitch on. He'd been in the shower."

"Well, of course," Blixen said. "In the buff."

"I beg your pardon?"

"Talking to myself. Okay. He confronted you. You panicked, ran downstairs with him right on your tail—"

Impatiently Lucille said: "Oh, let me tell it. You weren't there. You should have heard the man. Yelling, carrying on, you'd have thought I'd taken the crown jewels. Well, I had to defend myself. There was a butcher knife on the table in the kitchen, so I grabbed that on my way through. I begged him to stay away from me, but he followed me out to the yard. I don't think he saw the knife. He caught me at the edge of the drive." Her voice wavered. She cleared her throat, continued. "Nils, he was like a madman. So I stuck the knife in his belly and pushed." She lifted one hand absently. "Yet who would have thought the old man to have had so much blood in him?" she said.

Never had Blixen's lids felt so heavy. He decided to close them, just for a second, to shut out the stabbing light from the bedside lamp. "Yes," he said, "that was the key to it. One of the keys."

It threw her off her stride. The chair creaked. "Key?"

His body seemed to be drifting down a wide shaded stream, summer-warm, musical. "When I saw you that night at the ditch after the murder, you were blood from head to toe. Your dress and your nylons were drenched in blood."

"And that's the *key?*"

"What were you wearing when Clemmie woke you out of your sound nap?"

Lucille continued to gaze at him. "What *was* I wearing, Mr. Chan?"

"Jeans, probably," Blixen said. "Pants of some kind. Clem woke you up and carried you off to the Hamburger Hut, where you ran into Mick and his nosebleed. Remember telling me about that nosebleed? You said you reached into your pocket for a handkerchief, but Clemmie stopped you."

Lucille examined her fingers and gnawed at a hangnail.

"Not too many pockets in party dresses, are there," Blixen said.

"Which meant you'd changed your clothes. You'd had to. They were blood-soaked."

"Simply filthy," Lucille agreed. "I burned them later. I ran home and hid them and hauled out some clean jeans and jumped into those. Nobody noticed. Clemmie didn't." Grumpily she added: "I could have appeared in a celluloid collar and nothing else and Clemmie wouldn't have noticed. Neither would John."

"John? I thought it was Mick you ran into at the Hut?"

"John, Mick, who cares?"

"But you caused such a fuss about it—"

"I caused a *fuss,* Nils, so that you'd *note* the incident. Note that Sophocles had been there. I knew that Dwayne had identified the skeleton as Sophocles, and I wanted you and everybody else to realize that I couldn't possibly have killed him. I was with my boyfriend in Seaside at the time. I couldn't have cared less whether it was John you suspected, or Mick, or neither, okay?"

"Okay."

"Okay, then," Lucille grumped.

Blixen dozed, woke with a start. "Can we discuss poor John now? You killed him, too, didn't you? I see your arms are scratched. I presume that's why you were wearing the long-sleeved caftan the other night—"

"That's right, O great detective."

"Why was John such a danger to you?"

"Talk about your rotten luck," Lucille said. "You're really not going to believe this. Guess who came blundering in Friday with a toothache when Dwayne and I were kanoodling in his office?"

"So that's the doctor John had gone to! Heitkemper—"

"Why can't people make appointments! I just knew he'd cause trouble. I asked Dwayne to give him a little strychnine along with the codeine, but he wouldn't." Lucille brooded over her hangnail. "So sure enough, Saturday John calls me. What had Dwayne and I been doing? Were we lovers? Had we considered Clemmie's feelings? On and on. Well, I promised I'd run over and clarify the whole situation. I couldn't have him talking to Power. . . ." She sighed and plumped up her pillow. "Golly, just think of all the damage you could have prevented, Nils, if you'd remembered in the beginning that it was me you saw with the shovel that night. Why did you block it out, do you suppose?"

"Because my subconscious thought you were Karen."

"But weren't you and she together—?"

"She'd left the bedroom that night to go upstairs. When I woke, I was alone. I went looking for her—"

"And found a girl waving a bloody shovel over the DeForrest driveway—"

"Um . . . I was drunk. And I ran home and got even drunker. And that was the end of that memory."

"But it came back—"

"Just in flickers and flashes. As a matter of fact, the more I recalled, the muddier the waters got."

Lucille screwed up her forehead. "Muddier how?"

"Well," Blixen said, "for one thing the timing favored you. I saw a clock on Karen's dresser while I was still in bed. It was five minutes to one. The killer with the shovel couldn't have been you. You were in Seaside by then."

"How could you have been so mistaken about the time? It seems to me it was only a little after eleven when you came bumbling up the drive—"

"I wasn't mistaken. The clock said five minutes to one."

"Then it was two hours fast."

"No, it was absolutely accurate." Blixen resisted a yawn, cramped his feet. "It's just that I was observing it from the wrong angle."

"Well, I don't understand how angles could—"

"I remembered a light twitching and jumping in Karen's closet. But she swore she hadn't touched it. Drove me crazy. Until I saw my director's face swing around in the same way in Honolulu—in a cabinet mirror."

"Mirror—"

"I'd been looking into the full-length mirror on Karen's closet door. I remember thinking that I must have had eyes in the back of my head—because I could see the dresser behind me without turning. But it was a reflection I was seeing. The clock's hands didn't point to five minutes to one. They showed five minutes after eleven."

"Still," Lucille said, "I can't understand how you could have missed Sophocles. We could have sworn you spotted us both. . . ."

"I did. I thought he was the corpse—"

"No, no, darling, the corpse was under him. He was down there helping me—smoothing the dirt. He'd seen the whole thing. He came into the yard just as DeForrest caught me—"

"Then why didn't *he* call the police?"

"Because that wasn't his style," Lucille said. "Blackmail was his style. He said he'd help me. For a consideration. Well, I was in shock. I'd have agreed to anything. I even signed a little confession for him—"

"What was the consideration?"

"Not sex, darling, get your mind out of the gutter. He took the stickpin and the jewelry box."

"Ah."

"Then he buried the body. And then you came along. I wanted him to run after you and—and—what's the present tense of 'stove'?"

"Stave, I think."

"Stave your head in? Doesn't sound right. Well, he refused. He said one murder was enough for the neighborhood, and he doubted that you'd witnessed enough to matter anyway. I worried about it for a month or two and then I decided that we'd lucked out."

"How long did he blackmail you?"

"Oh, years. He hightailed it out of Portland that night, right after we all met him in the Hut, out of prudence, I suppose, and to leave me holding the bag in case you *had* seen something. He had a good deal of low cunning, Sophocles. Here's another example. He never demanded more than I could pay. Six or eight months would go by—years sometimes—and then I'd get a letter from Atlanta or South Dakota or somewhere, and I'd have to send twenty or thirty dollars to General Delivery. Just kept me dangling like that."

"Until this summer."

"What? Yes."

"He came back to Portland," Blixen went on, "in July or August—and he contacted you—"

"Very *good*," Lucille said admiringly. "You know that part, too."

"How much did he ask for this time?"

"Well, way too much, of course. He'd completely changed, Nils. All the cunning was gone. He called himself John W. Smith. He told me he lived out of garbage cans and soup kitchens, and that he was sick and tired of that environment, and he wanted me to give him ten thousand dollars so he could retire. Naturally I just laughed. I couldn't have scraped up ten thousand cents. Turns out he wasn't kidding. He still had my confession—he showed it to me—and he threatened to send it to Clemmie." She paused, plumped up the pillow again, rested her hands on it. "Whereupon I decided to kill him," she said.

Drowsily Blixen said: "You asked Heitkemper about the Slasher murders. He'd seen the bodies, knew the m.o.—"

"I didn't have to ask him. He'd been feeding me the gory details for weeks."

"You picked Sophocles up—"

"Yes, at the welfare office. I gave him a bottle of drugged wine to go with the sack of food they'd just handed him."

"Then once the wine had knocked him out, you took him into the West Hills to a house you knew was vacant, and you killed him in a fruit closet there."

"This is fascinating," Lucille said. "Tell me how I could be sure the house was vacant."

"Puzzled me for a while," Blixen answered, "until I remembered that you worked with Clemmie on the paper. In circulation. Whoever wanted to stop delivery for a month or two of vacation would have to notify you."

"Bingo," Lucille said. "Okay—killed him in the fruit closet—"

"And then," Blixen said, "you heard some terrible news. Clemmie mentioned that the police had arrested the Slasher a couple of days before. No way this new murder could be blamed on the Slasher if the Slasher was locked in a cell at the time—"

"Nils, I just went to pieces," Lucille said. "It's a wonder I didn't confess then and there. I'd almost lost my mind anyway when I was—you know—working on Sophocles. . . . Now I couldn't have him found. God knows where a new investigation would lead. I had to hide him, bury him. I'd kept the closet door unlocked. I pulled him out and buried him in the hills."

"But now," Blixen went on, "the kaleidoscope takes another couple of spins. Power decides he has the wrong man locked up.

The real Slasher could have done the latest murder after all. You decided to return the body to the fruit closet and go on with your original plan."

"Yeah, and this time I really jammed that door shut," Lucille said. "That way it would look like he'd been there all along."

Somnolently, Blixen said: "Dumb, Lucille."

It ruffled her feathers. "Well, it fooled Power. What was so dumb about it? There was blood all over the place. What would the owners have thought if they'd walked in to find all that blood and no body? Dumb, nothing."

"Lucille, it was dumb. You blew the whole shebang right there."

"How?"

"You remembered that Sophocles had had a sack with him—"

"Sure, I told you. A sack of food he'd scrounged at the welfare office."

"What happened to it?"

"I threw it away when I buried him. Couldn't find it when I went back—"

"You replaced it with new items—including a couple of potatoes—"

"Yes, I had to. I didn't want the police worrying about who he was. I knew some of the welfare people would connect the package with the man, and identify him as John W. Smith and that would be that, and I'd be off the hook. They'd figure the crazy Slasher had struck again."

"Very dumb."

"*Why?*"

"The body was supposed to have been locked up for three weeks—"

"Yes—"

"How long had the potatoes been locked up?"

"Who'd care? Or know?"

"I knew. I saw it when I was talking to Power at your place. Clemmie said something about the corpse that had spent three glorious weeks in the fruit closet."

"Well?"

"But the potatoes hadn't spent three weeks there. They were just three plain potatoes."

"I can't—"

"Lucille, think. What would three potatoes have done in three weeks in the dark?"

After a moment Lucille said: "Sprouted." Sighing, she shut her eyes, tapped her fingernails against her front teeth. "Sprouted, sprouted, sprouted," she said.

"The potatoes were fresh," Blixen said, "which meant that they —and the body—had just been dumped there. Somebody was going to a lot of trouble to blame this new murder on the Slasher. I began to wonder why."

Lazily, Blixen listened to his own voice drone away like a summer bee on a clover blossom, intermittent, afternoonish, meaningless. He gave a start. Lucille had touched his shoulder.

"Nils, are you asleep?"

He dragged his lids up. "Certainly not."

"But you're tired, I can see that." The pillow floated above his face. "Poor tired lad. . . ."

"Lucille, you're too late," Blixen said. "Look behind you."

"Oh, darling, television has done your mind a mischief. Didn't that trick go out with 'Maverick'?"

"Did it, Sergeant?" Blixen asked.

"There's no trick like an old trick," Power said from the doorway.

The pillow hung motionless.

"Thank heaven I wasn't hallucinating," Blixen said.

Softly Lucille said: "Sergeant Power, how long have you been out there?"

"Ever since you walked in. We wondered why you'd come in the back way, onto a floor that had been marked off limits to all visitors."

After a time, Lucille said: "If you planned to guard the man, why didn't you place a policeman in the hall?"

"Same reason I keep my tape recorder in a glove compartment. I hate to inhibit the guilty."

"I don't expect the Supreme Court would find that very amusing."

"No, ma'am, I expect not."

"What I don't find very amusing," Blixen said, "is the fact that this lunatic could have whapped that pillow down on my face while you were out there recording away."

"We'd have been on her in a flash," Power assured him.

"What do you mean, lunatic?" Lucille said.

"Don't fight it, lady," Power advised. "I can guarantee you that that passion plea would have about as much chance as a snowflake on a stove."

"Oh," Lucille said. "Right." Presently she lowered the pillow and put it on the chair and sat on it like a little girl. She played with her fingers and hummed to herself.

"Okay, Swinnerton," Power called, and the human pillbox rolled in and read Lucille Gompers her rights and hustled her away while Power stood over the bed and explained to Blixen how he would now go and charge Heitkemper as an accessory, none of which Blixen saw or heard or cared about.

Because Blixen was asleep.

CHAPTER FOURTEEN

L'envoi

By Tuesday he felt grouchy enough to crab about the gruel they offered him for breakfast and to snap at the nurse who changed his dressing, so somebody in charge decided that he must be more or less on the road to recovery and that he probably could tolerate official visitors now.

His first official visitor—wouldn't you know it—turned out to be Detective Sergeant Conrad Power.

Blixen was muttering back at some TV soap opera heroine when Power stuck his big nose around the door and said: "Are you busy?"

"Oh, Lord, you again?" Blixen groaned, and Power said in a rather hurt tone that he could sense when he wasn't wanted and therefore he and his companion would just mosey along, and Blixen asked what companion? and Karen appeared beneath Power's nose and Blixen not only improved, he felt like singing.

"Hi," Karen said.

"Hi," said Blixen.

The gypsy shirt and the jeans were gone, and she was in gym shorts and running shoes and a baggy, long-sleeved sweat shirt that said THURSDAY NIGHT LADIES KNITTING AND TERRORIST SOCI-ETY across the chest.

Her loveliness clutched like a hand at Blixen's throat.

"Well," she said, and spread her arms. "I'm free."

"Yes." Blixen glanced at Power, back at Karen. "By the way, how's your scratched arm?"

"Oh, fine." She pushed the sleeve up to show him. "Cat claws never go very deep." She tilted her head toward Power. "Sherlock Holmes here thought MacVicar had scratched me in his death throes. Can you imagine?"

"Unbelievable," Blixen said.

After a moment Karen said shyly: "And how's your bullet wound?"

"Oh—much better."

"The doctor said it was. He said you'd be going home in a day or two." She moved closer. "Does your face hurt?"

"My—no. . . . Just my belly."

"Then I won't kiss your belly." She bent to him, touched her cool lips to his cheek. "Oh, Nils," she whispered, "I'm going to miss you so terribly. . . ."

Blixen said: "Well—Karen—there's no need. If you'll come with me—"

It caught them both by surprise.

Drawing back, Karen said: "What?"

"I think," Blixen said, "that I just asked for your hand in marriage. Will you?"

Karen glanced from side to side and Power pushed a chair over for her to sit down in, and Karen said: "Well, for pity's sake."

"Never rains but it pours, does it?" Power said, and to Blixen: "Look at her ring finger."

Karen raised it. The diamond was barely there, but it did glitter. "Gogarty," she said.

"Gogarty!"

"Nils, it's your own fault. You were the teacher. You said: 'Trust. Depend.' You said: 'Swim—' "

"But I didn't say swim to Gogarty!"

"But that's who I'd been trying to swim to for years. So when he asked me again yesterday . . ." Briskly she patted his cheek. "Now don't sulk. We'll come visit you in Hollywood. You'll love Gogarty."

"Out!" Blixen said. "Out! Out!" Although when she tried to rise, he caught her hand and then held it to his cheek and then kissed the palm of it.

"Darling," Karen whispered, "thank you so very, very much . . . for everything. . . ."

Power had gone to stand in the open doorway.

Karen freed herself, walked to Power, and paused uncertainly. "By the way, Sheriff," she said, "who *was* that Masked Man—?"

"Well, ma'am," Power told her, "nobody really knows his name. But around here, folks call him the—"

They were gone.

Smiling, Blixen thought: *Yes, that's the right ending. You'll be happy, love.*

Trust me.

About the Author

Charles Larson wrote for the pulp magazines until 1943 when he was put under contract as a screenwriter for MGM. He began writing for television in 1951 and began producing for television in 1964. He has produced four seasons of "The FBI," "The Interns," and "Cade's County." He has written two books for the Crime Club featuring Nils Blixen, *Muir's Blood* and *Matthew's Hand,* and produced the "Tuesday Night Movie" for CBS called *The Crime Club*. He and his wife live in Portland, Oregon.